Brooke wished this baby she carried belonged to Oliver.

Don't you start weaving plans around him. They were friends with benefits. That's what they'd both agreed on, and she aimed to stick by her word.

She sighed. Being honorable was such a burden.

"You okay?" Oliver stroked her hair.

She wanted to purr like a kitten. "Better than okay. You?"

"Phenomenal."

She snuggled against him. She had to face the truth, even though she couldn't act on it.

She'd fallen in love with Oliver. No telling when or how it had happened, or whether she could have prevented it.

What that meant for her future and for the baby, she had no idea. But she had to acknowledge that it had become impossible to find Mr. Right.

Because she'd already found him.

Dear Reader,

No matter how carefully an author plans, when she sits down to write she never really knows how a book will take shape.

For me, Brooke jumped off the page from the start. Naively optimistic and generous of spirit, she proved wise beyond her years. As for Oliver, he might be a bit of a cynic, but he and Brooke lit up my computer screen. I had a great time with them.

You'll also meet Sherry LaSalle, an heiress with a tendency to fall for the wrong man, and Rafe Montoya, a mechanic who considers her a hopeless snob. They're as unlikely a couple as I've created in more than eighty novels, and their story, MILLION-DOLLAR NANNY, will be published in early 2009.

Best,

Jacqueline Diamond

Baby in Waiting

JACQUELINE DIAMOND

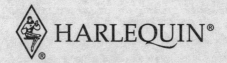

TORONTO • NEW YORK • LONDON
AMSTERDAM • PARIS • SYDNEY • HAMBURG
STOCKHOLM • ATHENS • TOKYO • MILAN • MADRID
PRAGUE • WARSAW • BUDAPEST • AUCKLAND

ISBN-13: 978-0-373-75227-0
ISBN-10:   0-373-75227-X

BABY IN WAITING

ABOUT THE AUTHOR

An author of eighty novels, Jacqueline Diamond enjoys blending humor with stories about people growing and exploring their lives. She lives in a Southern California community a lot like Harmony Circle, where people fall in love, fall out of love, have babies, make friends and struggle to raise their children. She enjoys hearing from readers at Jdiamondfriends@yahoo.com and posts her latest news and views on her Web site, www.jacquelinediamond.com.

Books by Jacqueline Diamond

HARLEQUIN AMERICAN ROMANCE

To Donna Hendricks, a writer in waiting

Chapter One

Brooke Bernard returned from lunch to find every parking spot in the Archway Center occupied. Leaving her car on the street wouldn't have bothered her except for the fact that two prime spaces right in front of Smile Central, where she worked as a receptionist, were occupied by a single gas-guzzling luxury car that belonged to a man with an ego the size of an oil refinery.

Oliver Armstrong.

On this particular Monday she was in no mood to tolerate such arrogance. Particularly not from a guy who'd recently broken up with her best friend, Renée Trent, who worked next door at the Hair Apparent beauty salon. Renée and Oliver both claimed that they'd drifted apart, but Brooke found it hard to believe. Egotistical as he might be, Oliver was extremely good-looking, and Renée had been fond of him.

Today was his unlucky day, because Brooke really, really wanted to give some man, any man, a piece of her mind, and with his thoughtless act of parking piracy, Oliver had made himself an obvious candidate. Also, Brooke needed to spend the rest of her lunch break checking out the bulletin board at the Archway Real Estate office, which Oliver owned. She might as well confront him while she was there.

After hiking a block and half from her car to the Archway Center, Brooke was huffing a bit hard for a twenty-five-year-old woman. She couldn't blame the weather, which was as clear and crisp as one might expect for mid-March in Southern California. She blamed Oliver for that, as well.

She stalked into Archway Real Estate ablaze with righteous indignation, only to discover that the front desk was unoccupied and the agents in their cubicles paid her no heed. To complete her sense of anticlimax, she could see Oliver through the glass front of his private office conferring with a couple of people who appeared to be clients.

Showdown postponed.

Pushing her sunglasses up onto her head, Brooke shifted her attention to the printed fliers and hand-lettered notices pinned to the bulletin board. A lost poodle, a litter of free kittens, college students tutoring math. Where were all the renters seeking roommates?

The last time she'd checked there'd been zillions of possibilities. Still, that was ages ago. She supposed most people moved at the start or end of the school year.

An ad for a home to lease caught her eye. Three bedrooms, fresh paint, large kitchen… While the rent seemed exorbitant to her, it was in line with prices here in the upscale town of Brea. Brooke happened to know that the house, located on the street Renée lived on, belonged to Oliver. He rented it out and lived in another of his properties, a luxury condo in the center of town. Must be nice to own more houses than you needed.

Well, she didn't require fancy digs *or* a guy who'd sell his best friend for a profit. Brooke preferred simple places and people who cared about each other.

Also, at present, people who had a room for rent—because she needed one, badly.

The door to Oliver's office swung open and he ushered his clients out. Where'd he gotten the sharp new haircut that made his dark hair seem even thicker? Had he switched salons after parting ways with Renée?

As Oliver and his visitors headed in her direction, Brooke pretended to be fascinated with the bulletin board. Her back turned, she listened to the two clients thanking Oliver. His smooth words assured them that they'd made the right choice by listing their house with him.

In the window Brooke could see reflected handshakes and farewells. And then she registered the moment when Oliver spotted her. An unwelcome tingle ran along her spine.

"Hey." He stopped at her side. "What brings you here?"

Brooke swung around, refusing to be cowed by his height or distracted by those sea-blue eyes. "You're hogging two spaces."

"Who, me?"

His pretense of innocence fueled her indignation. "I had to walk a block and a half because of you."

"My apologies." He didn't exactly sound contrite. "Still, you can't assume the space would have stayed empty till you got there."

"Of all the ridiculous—"

"Also, my client uses a cane, in case you didn't notice. I had to leave him room to get out. Since I'm only staying a few minutes, I figured, why waste gas by shifting the car?"

Brooke hated logic. People who stole parking spaces shouldn't be forgiven, no matter what excuse they used.

"Who cut your hair?" she demanded.

He grinned. "Renée. Why do you refuse to believe we're still friends? She told me you're gunning for my hide."

"I am not. I…" She halted.

"It's just that all men are jerks," he filled in for her. "Right?"

"You should know."

Oliver's grin widened. "What's he done now?"

Brooke folded her arms, embarrassed. Thank goodness none of the other agents was close enough to overhear. "If you're referring to Kevin…."

"Your true love, the one who sold you a song and dance about how his wife threw him out and begged you to let him move in with you? If I can recall all the details of this soap opera, he's also the one who showered you with gifts he charged to a friend's credit card. A friend who happens to be your boss."

"He paid Dr. Salonica back. Besides, they weren't gifts, plural. Just a bouquet of roses." The men—both in their forties—were golfing buddies who often did each other favors. Her boss, who was an orthodontist, had allowed the charge because Kevin didn't want his wife to find out he was having an affair during their separation.

"And he omitted to tell you that he has two little girls, and that he was the one who chose to play hooky."

"He…" Brooke halted. Kevin Corcoran deserved no excuses. He'd created a mess for her *and* for his family. "Okay, I'm ticked off at him."

"What's his latest transgression?" Oliver persisted.

She averted her gaze. "He and his wife are reconciling."

"I'm sorry to hear it. I mean, for your sake."

The last thing she sought was sympathy. "It's a good thing. I mean, because of their daughters." Brooke didn't especially care to admit that she'd spent the entire weekend sobbing into a pillow. She *did* hope the couple reunited. "The problem is, now I have to find a place to live."

"What's wrong with your apartment?"

This was the most painful part. "Kevin insisted on handling the rent while he was living with me. I gave him my half every month, but somehow he got behind."

"Somehow?" Oliver pressed.

She hated to think the worst of a man she'd trusted. He had been fun to be around, impulsive and admiring. And for a while he'd filled a hole in her life. "He had to support his kids and…okay, that's no excuse. Anyway, yesterday the landlord served me a three-day pay-or-quit notice. The bottom line is, I have to be out by tomorrow."

Oliver glowered. "That lout stole your money? Somebody ought to teach him a lesson."

"Don't go pounding him!" Brooke begged. "You wouldn't, would you?"

He shrugged. "No, but you should insist he bring the rent up-to-date. From what I hear, he has a good job as an insurance agent."

"He means well. But it's hard supporting two households." So Kevin had told her repeatedly.

"Let me guess. He claims that if you press him for the money, you'll be hurting his family."

She winced. "Let's not go there. I don't suppose you've heard of anybody looking for a house-sitter? That would save me a bundle."

Oliver's scowl vanished. "This is what I love about

you, Brooke. Your life may be a disaster, but nothing keeps you down."

"There's something about me you love?" she shot back. "That's news."

"Why not? You're entertaining. Kind of like watching a ten-car pileup on the freeway," Oliver teased. "And since I'm in such a benevolent mood, I'll ask around about house-sitting. Meanwhile, why don't you stay with Renée? She has three bedrooms."

"I hate imposing on friends."

"You asked *me* to find you a free place to live."

"Since when are we friends?"

Oliver chuckled. "I see your point."

With a cheerful wave, Brooke whisked out the door and into her office. As she took her place behind the desk at Smile Central, she wondered if any of the nice moms in the waiting room might like a live-in nanny who was available evenings and weekends. That would solve her housing problem, and she loved kids. She couldn't very well inquire without endangering her job, however. And her job was already on shaky ground.

The problem was the dozen roses that Kevin had charged to Dr. Salonica's credit card. The orthodontist's wife, Helen, had spotted the charge, traced the flower delivery to Brooke's address and then had accused her own husband of courting the receptionist. Flustered, he claimed he'd sent them because Brooke's mother died.

Well, she *had* died. Ten years earlier.

Since then Helen had dropped by Smile Central twice to snoop, but she'd found no further cause for suspicion. Of course not. The very idea of passion flaring between Brooke and her pudgy, balding boss was preposterous.

Now, if she could just find a place to stay. Worst-case scenario, she might have to sleep in her car for a while. It wouldn't be the first time.

No use worrying—something would turn up. It always did.

FOR OLIVER, Mondays were a juggling act. As were Tuesdays, Wednesdays, Thursdays, Fridays and Saturdays. What had he forgotten? Oh, yes, Sundays, too. And when he wasn't selling houses, he was supervising the ten agents who worked at his brokerage.

He got his exercise walking door-to-door, distributing fliers and chatting up potential clients, and he generally ate on the run. The exception was the rare occasion he joined Renée and Brooke at the sandwich shop that was located two stores down. Renée had been a charming companion for a while, and Brooke amused him with her flyaway cinnamon hair, her infectious laughter and her positive, carefree approach to life.

He'd never met anyone so completely different from himself. Growing up the middle child of financially strained parents, Oliver had always had a determination to accomplish two things: to amass investment capital and to become a major player in the business world by the age of thirty-five.

At thirty-one, he'd made numerous legitimate strides in that direction. The problem with owning a business and properties, however, was that they ate huge quantities of money. On paper, he looked great. But in practice, cashflow crunches made this nonstop juggling act of his a necessity.

Adding to the pressure was a breakthrough opportunity

that he'd just set his sights on. Not quite on a par with, say, Microsoft just before it released Windows, but the best shot he was liable to have for a long while.

After checking around the office to see if anyone needed a house-sitter—and no one did—Oliver picked up his laptop and headed out. En route, he put in a call to Renée, who was at home, since the salon was closed on Mondays.

"I just stepped out of the shower," she told him coolly. "If this isn't urgent, I'd prefer to call you back."

"It won't take long." He described Brooke's situation.

As he spoke to Renée, he tried not to think about how sensational the willowy blonde must look in her delicate silk wrapper—if she wore even that much. Renée definitely was his type, yet they'd lost interest in each other after a few months of dating. Oliver supposed that was partly because of his schedule, but he'd also gotten a strong sense that Renée backed away from real intimacy. No hard feelings on either side.

"I could strangle Kevin!" she responded. "I wish Brooke had told me."

"She thought that would be taking advantage." Cell phone pressed to his ear, Oliver stood beside his car.

"She can certainly stay here for a couple of weeks, until my remodeling starts." Since she'd bought her house the previous fall, Renée had been busy working out a color scheme and selecting tile, carpet and appliances. "Once Josh tears up my kitchen and pulls out the carpets, there'll be fibers and fumes everywhere."

Contractor Josh Lorenz, who lived across the street from Renée, had a long list of clients, all admirers of his high-quality workmanship. His current projects included the restoration of Oliver's rental. The former renters, who'd recently moved to Nevada, had been famous for their loud power tools, cluttered porch and noisy teenagers. When they moved out, they left the house in bad shape.

Oliver beeped his car open. A motorcycle had slid into the remaining half space, so at least Brooke's inconvenience had turned out to be another person's good luck. "Where are *you* going to stay?"

"With a neighbor, Tess Phipps. She's the divorce attorney."

"I remember when she bought that house. Nice lady." Oliver had a passing acquaintance with most of the home owners in the Harmony Circle development. The comfortable enclave, set among Brea's northern hills, offered its more than three hundred residents a pool, a playground and a clubhouse, where monthly potlucks were held. Its communal atmosphere made an excellent selling point.

"I hope Brooke can find another place to stay by then," Renée said anxiously. "I can't ask Tess to put her up, too."

Oliver positioned the phone in a holder and affixed a hands-free headset before switching on the ignition. "I'm sure she will." That little scatterbrain had a knack for landing on her feet.

"I'm surprised you're interested in helping her. I thought altruism wasn't your style."

"It isn't." Having fought his way to success on his own, he figured that if he could do it so could others. In his opinion, when an able-bodied person stuck out his hand, someone ought to slap a job application into it right away. Brooke, however, hadn't asked for charity. "Besides, *I'm* not the one taking her in."

Renée laughed. "Altruism's okay, as long as I'm doing it?"

"No reason she can't pay rent while she's there." He checked before backing out of the space. Or, to be precise, the space and a half.

"I'd rather she saved the money for a deposit," she replied. "That creep Kevin sucked her dry. She even paid for their food."

Instead of sympathy, Oliver felt a twist of irritation. He considered gullibility a character flaw. "Let's hope she learned a lesson."

"I kind of hope she doesn't learn too many lessons." Renée sounded wistful. "For all her hard knocks, she's still bighearted and trusting. I'd hate to see that change."

"Would you rather see her go through life getting ripped off?" He halted at the curb, waiting for traffic to clear. "Hey, I've got a call coming in. Catch you later."

"Ciao."

The caller turned out to be Josh Lorenz. He'd just stopped by Oliver's empty rental to check on the painter. "He suggested adding blue trim to the exterior," Josh reported. "I realize you'd have to request a waiver to the home owners' guidelines, but it would certainly look sharp."

The neighborhood association restricted exterior colors to a range of earth tones. "Great. Another reason to make everyone resent me." Oliver eased the car into traffic.

"Everyone doesn't resent you," Josh protested.

"Oh, yeah? Name three who don't."

"Me. Renée. Mmm…" Josh got stuck.

"There you go."

Until a few months ago, Oliver had been a popular guy. Then he'd sold a historic cottage—one of a pair grandfathered into the otherwise modern development—to a wealthy couple who wanted to tear it down.

Their plans to build a mansion were now wending their way through the city's review process. And most of Harmony Circle was up in arms. Even Oliver's cousin, Rafe, who lived opposite the cottage, barely spoke to Oliver these days.

"I'll tell the painter no," Josh said. "Catch you later."

"Thanks."

Oliver clicked off. Although he owned property in Harmony Circle, thank goodness he didn't have to live in the midst of all that domesticity—and antagonism. He preferred his condo, which was within walking distance of the town's movie theaters, comedy club and restaurants.

He did wish the swinging bachelors in the condo next door would stop leaving their barbecue unattended on their deck. Since they also leashed their dog out there, the situation struck him as a disaster waiting to happen.

Anyway, he'd talk to his neighbors about that tonight. Or as soon as he found the time.

The rest of the day flew by. Around 7:00 p.m. Oliver was eating a hamburger at his desk when another agent stuck his head through the door and asked, "Any idea what's going on?"

"Sorry?"

"The sirens."

Without realizing it, Oliver had been listening to the noise for several minutes. Serious crime was unusual in Brea, where a crime wave was never anything more than teenagers shoplifting at the mall.

"There's a lot of smoke rising over the downtown area."

Out front on the walkway Oliver joined a knot of people staring over the rooftops at a dense plume of smoke about a mile off. "That's weird," somebody said. "We don't usually get brush fires in March."

"We don't get brush fires in the middle of downtown, either," someone else cracked.

Oliver began to have a bad feeling.

He leaped into his car and took a shortcut home, skirting the main thoroughfare. At his condo complex, he halted amid a tangle of fire trucks and hoses.

A firefighter approached the car. "How'd you get past the safety barrier?"

Oliver rolled down his window, grateful that he'd stuck to back streets. "I didn't see one. I live here. What happened?"

"A dog knocked over somebody's barbecue."

"Was the dog hurt?"

"It's fine. Sir, you need to move your car."

"Sure." Despite his anxiety, he figured he'd better comply. After parking a few dozen feet away, clear of the hoses, Oliver jumped out to see just how much damage one dog and one barbecue had caused.

When he glimpsed the blackened remains of the shared structure, his initial bad feeling mushroomed into a full-blown cloud of dismay. The place would have to be rebuilt from the ground up. He'd lost all his entertainment equipment, his furniture and his clothes. Worse than that, he had no choice but to move into his empty rental house, right in the middle of a bunch of angry neighbors.

Maybe he should install bulletproof glass.

Chapter Two

Early Sunday afternoon, Brooke sat on Renée's rear patio, intending to paint her toenails and catch a few rays in her bikini. Unable to relax, she looked around and concluded that the stucco garden wall and high bushes made this place a little too isolated. Renée had driven off the night before on a jaunt to Las Vegas, and Brooke already missed her company.

She pulled the lounge chair onto the front lawn. Much better.

Renée's elevated corner lot provided an excellent view of the Spanish-style houses that lined horseshoe-shaped Harmony Road. Toward the bend in the road, a couple of children raced about, playing tag.

In the five days since she'd moved in, Brooke had met many of the neighbors. She hoped some of them might stop by to chat.

Propping her right foot on a cushion, she uncapped a bottle of Slay Me Red. But the sharp scent instantly made her stomach churn—which was odd, because she loved the smell of nail polish. It always reminded her of junior high, when she and her mom had shared makeup tips and painted each other's nails. She wished she'd appreciated how precious those moments had been.

Bending forward, Brooke experienced another queasy sensation. She hoped that meant her period was about to arrive. Amid the turmoil of moving, she'd lost track of her body and hadn't realized until yesterday that she was late.

At Renée's insistence, she'd bought a pregnancy kit, but she hadn't made use of it yet. What a waste of money. No baby would be crazy enough to pick a mother like Brooke, who couldn't think beyond next weekend.

Besides, that kind of news might shatter Kevin's tentative accord with his wife. If Laura found out that her husband had had an affair, let alone impregnated another woman…well, she'd kick him out for good, which would break their little girls' hearts.

Oh, pooh. Nothing to worry about. Although Brooke and Kevin had taken a few risks with their lovemaking, half the women she knew were undergoing treatment for infertility. What were the odds of becoming pregnant by accident?

She'd better stop thinking about this or she'd smear the polish. In fact, she'd already done so.

Grumbling, Brooke dabbed away the errant color with a paper towel. She must have been distracted, because she didn't notice anyone approaching until she heard a man's voice from half a dozen feet away.

"That might be easier if you took off your sunglasses," he said.

She peered up at Oliver Armstrong. Bright sunlight washed out all subtleties of shape and texture even as it emphasized his powerful build, and her sunglasses turned his eyes an intriguing turquoise. "Where'd you come from?"

"I was dropping off some escrow papers nearby and what to my wondering eyes should appear but Brooke Bernard, on display for the whole world to admire."

He inspected her shape with what appeared to be detached appreciation. All the same a prickly sensation stole across her skin, accompanied by unwelcome warmth.

Brooke adjusted her sunglasses and replied with as much aplomb as she could muster, "As far as I can tell, you're the only person who's noticed me. So, how're things going? Have you moved in yet?"

All week long the Archway Center had been abuzz with news of the fire. According to the local newspaper, four condo units had been gutted and rebuilding was expected to take as long as a year. According to an agent from Oliver's office, he'd spent the week at a hotel, courtesy of his insurance company, and he planned to relocate to the rental house in the immediate future.

Too bad his beach cottage was an hour and a half away, or he could have consoled himself with morning dips in the surf. Poor guy.

"Renée didn't reach you?" Oliver asked.

"What do you mean, reach me?"

"I guess not. What'd you do, forget to charge your cell phone?"

"Uh…" So *that* was why it hadn't rung since yesterday. "Must have."

Oliver gestured toward Harmony Road. "If you'll squint through those sunglasses… They're hideous, by the way. Why pink flamingos?"

"A friend sent them from Florida," Brooke informed him. "For my collection."

"Of sunglasses?"

"What else?"

He crouched low for a closer look. "If you have a collection, you *must* own another pair that's better than these."

"I rotate them. It seems only fair."

"They're inanimate objects, Brooke. They don't care whether you wear them."

"*I* care."

"Anyway, if you'll focus those monstrosities on my house, you'll notice something interesting."

Peering between the neighboring houses, she spotted the billowing stripes of a tent. "You're staging a circus?"

"A circus for termites," Oliver said. "A farewell party."

"Oh." Hiring exterminators must be expensive. "You've sure had a run of bad luck. What'd you do, tick off a Gypsy?"

"Here's the thing," he murmured close to her ear. "I can't take occupancy until Tuesday."

The scent of peppermint on his breath had a heady effect. Brooke countered it by leaning forward to blow on her toenails. "You'll have to hang out a while longer at the Embassy Suites. Whirlpool bath, cable TV and a fresh-cooked breakfast—what a rough life."

"Sad to say, the insurance company is done footing the bill for that. You'll excuse my reference to feet, right? I mean, since you're waving yours in my face."

"Am not!" Brooke glared. "What're you doing here, anyway?"

He rose and brushed off his slacks. "Picking out a bedroom."

She tried to digest this information. "Renée's letting you stay here?" The woman must have lost her mind.

"Until Tuesday. I'm swapping her for a free weekend

at the beach." He rented out his beachfront place on a weekly basis.

"But she isn't even here." How could Renée leave Brooke alone with Oliver? This was awkward and maddening.

At least she wouldn't be lonely. She supposed the situation had its redeeming aspects.

"Don't worry. You'll hardly know I'm around." He smirked. "Renée said there's a spare key in the kitchen drawer. Don't bother getting up—I'll use the rear entrance."

As he started around the house, Brooke visualized her pregnancy kit resting on the bathroom counter. Oliver couldn't miss it when he used the facilities. "Wait!"

"I promise not to steal anything," his answer drifted back.

Brooke capped the polish, swung off the lounger and crossed the expanse of grass. Elevating her freshly painted toes, she adopted an awkward hopping gait that probably looked ridiculous. Darn the man, anyway.

A series of thumps later, she bounced through the rear door and into the den. In the center stood Oliver, surveying an array of teddy bears perched on various chairs and tables. "Another collection of yours?"

"Yep." She considered ways to slip past him without being obvious or risking body contact. Didn't seem possible. Bowling him over might do the trick, although it lacked subtlety.

He cocked his head. "Interesting, the way you've got them wearing sunglasses. Good place to store them."

"If you're in the mood for a cuddle, the bears are available." Straightening a strap on her bikini top, she took a step forward. "I have other things to do."

He shifted into her path as if by accident. "How many of these were gifts from Kevin?"

"Three or four. Why do you care?"

"Just curious. Speaking of lover boy, have you asked him for the money he owes you?"

She'd spoken to Kevin briefly on Wednesday. "He can't. His wife keeps tabs on his checkbook and credit-card receipts."

"He never told her he was living with you?"

"No, and…" She halted. It was best to keep a lock on her tongue. Although Oliver already knew that Kevin had once borrowed Dr. Salonica's charge card, he'd *really* have something to say if he learned how much trouble those flowers were causing.

Helen Salonica, former model who was one of Orange County's social elite, had swept through the office the previous Friday and fixed Brooke with a murderous glare. She still didn't buy her husband's explanation.

Right now, Brooke had a more immediate challenge—getting past Oliver. Since he seemed determined to provoke her, she opted for the blunt approach. "I have to use the bathroom."

"Don't let me stop you."

"You're in my way. "

"What? Oh. Sorry." Lazily, Oliver stepped back a few inches.

Passing him, Brooke couldn't avoid bumping him. Through the crisp slacks, his thigh felt solid and… scorching. Annoyed with him and with herself, she hurried down the hall.

Once in the bathroom, she shut the door. The kit sat on the counter, as obvious as could be. Where to stash it? She didn't dare carry it to her bedroom, since Oliver might be out there watching. Instead, she bent down and stuck it beneath the sink, behind a bottle of toilet cleaner.

Safe as in a bank vault. Men *never* cleaned the bathroom.

When she emerged, Oliver was inspecting the third bedroom, which held Renée's sewing machine and a stack of boxes. "There's no bed in here."

"She stores a futon in the garage."

"I'll take the master bedroom. It's not as if I haven't slept there before."

Renée *had* given him permission to stay. "You're leaving on Tuesday, right? Where are you going to sleep Monday after she gets home?"

He angled himself in the doorway. "Maybe she misses me?"

Brooke wouldn't blame Renée. These two ought to get back together. They suited each other in a lot of ways.

A traitorous wisp of envy curled through her stomach. She ignored it. "That's her choice."

"How about you? Found another place yet?" he asked. "Renée's renovations start in a week, as I recall."

"I'm going to share a place with the other dental receptionist and her brother." Because of a recent rent raise, Faye and her sibling had decided to seek a roommate.

"Her brother?" he repeated. "What's he like?"

"Dougie's kind of a nerd." Neither he nor Faye gave off the greatest vibes. Nor was Brooke crazy about the fact that although she would have to pay half the rent, she would be sharing one of the two bedrooms with Faye.

Still, they were allowing her to join them and they were waiving a deposit.

"Glad things worked out." Oliver ducked into Renée's

room with Brooke on his heels. "Would you put away that nightgown she left on the bed? Since we broke up, I don't think I should handle her personal stuff."

"You don't consider sleeping between her sheets personal?"

"I'll wash them before she gets home."

"How considerate."

As Brooke carried the silk nightie to the closet, she wished she wasn't so aware of being alone in a bedroom with Oliver. For Pete's sake, this was her closest friend's ex-boyfriend, a guy who swaggered when he walked.

Kind of a cute, pirate-type swagger. He did have great hips, too. A woman couldn't help noticing these things.

How embarrassing to feel her breath coming faster than normal. Brooke cast a sideways glance to see if Oliver had noticed.

Their gazes locked. His chest rose and fell heavily. Oh, yes, he'd noticed.

With an amused shrug, he indicated the bureau. "I'd appreciate it if you'd tuck her cosmetics into a drawer."

Miffed for reasons she didn't quite understand, Brooke stood her ground. "If you're not planning to handle her stuff, where are you going to put your clothes?"

"She kept an empty drawer and space in her closet for me while we were dating. They're still there."

She went cold. "She's saving them for you."

"Doubtful. I presume they're for her next gentleman."

"Then you should ask if it's okay to sleep in here!" Brooke retorted. If Oliver had to sleep in the living room, he might decide to find other quarters.

"You're right." He whipped out his cell phone. "I'll take care of it right now."

A short conversation later, he flashed Brooke a thumbs-up. Too bad. Didn't Renée realize how impossible this situation was?

Well, how could she? When Brooke and Oliver had been thrown into each other's company during his relationship with Renée, they'd exchanged playful taunts but had left it at that.

It was no big deal, Brooke thought. None at all.

After exchanging a few pleasantries, he clicked off. "She sends apologies for not telling you about our arrangement. She tried to get through on your phone."

"She doesn't owe me an apology," Brooke replied, pulling herself together. "It's a big favor letting *me* stay here."

Oliver frowned. "That doesn't mean she shouldn't take your feelings into consideration."

Nonsense. "This is her house and she's entitled to invite the Mighty Ducks to stay here if it suits her." Renée was a fan of the Stanley Cup-winning hockey team that was based in nearby Anaheim.

"She's dating a hockey player?" he asked in surprise.

"Would you mind?"

"No. If she had a connection like that, I'd try to work out a publicity arrangement. Feature them in my ads in exchange for tickets for clients. Maybe sell them a few houses." He beamed at the notion.

"You wouldn't be jealous?" Brooke didn't understand.

"She's free to date whoever she likes."

What an unsatisfying answer! Rather than dwell on the subject, she said, "Need help bringing things from your car?"

"That would be great."

Brooke expected to find the sedan packed to the roof.

But when Oliver opened the trunk, all she saw was a laptop case, a suitcase and a hanging bag of clothes. Plus half a dozen Open House signs. "That's it?"

He laid the clothes bag across her arms. "Most of my possessions got fried."

After shutting the trunk, he carried the luggage along the walkway. Brooke hurried to keep up. "Your insurance is replacing everything, right?"

He held the door for her. "Who can remember all the things they own? I'm sure I left half my DVDs and videogames off the list, and I keep remembering other odds and ends."

"I never thought of that."

"At least they pay replacement value for the furniture and electronics."

Brooke hadn't considered how complicated it could be to deal with the aftermath of a fire. "I'll bet you lost a lot of stuff that had sentimental value."

"You mean, like scrapbooks and heirlooms? I don't have any," Oliver told her as they made their way through the house. "I keep my documents in a safe-deposit box and my records are all in my laptop."

She was glad he hadn't lost anything irreplaceable. Under the circumstances, it seemed pointless to take pity on him. In some ways, his situation might even be enviable. "If I were you, I'd indulge myself. Stay in a hotel as long as I could, even if I had to pay the tab out of my own pocket. Why not, if you've got the money?"

He transferred his clothes to the closet, careful to avoid wrinkling them. "Ever heard of watching your expenses and saving for the future?"

"In theory," she admitted.

"Didn't anyone ever talk to you about financial planning?"

A waste of energy to worry about the future, Brooke mused. "Why bother? I could get hit by a truck tomorrow."

"Or you could live to be ninety," he pointed out. "Ninety and broke. Happens to a lot of people who think the way you do."

Unfazed, Brooke said, "I'll deal with that if and when I get there."

"It'll be too late then."

"Maybe I'll win the lottery."

Oliver groaned. "You're hopeless."

"I'm hope*ful*," she corrected. "Unlike you, Mr. I'm-Such-a-Pessimist-I-Can-Hardly-Stand-It."

That startled him. "Interesting perspective. I'm a pessimist because I think you might live to be ninety. Look, I'd love to continue this heart-to-heart, but I have to pick up snacks for an open house."

Brooke should have realized he'd be working, weekend or not. Disappointment clouded her mood until she recalled that he was staying here. Which meant he'd be back tonight and she'd have someone to cook for. "We can talk over dinner."

"Don't bother to fix anything for me. I'll just munch on some snacks." He transferred a neat folded stack of garments from suitcase to drawer.

"What kind of snacks?" she asked.

"Cookies. Doughnuts."

"Those aren't dinner! How do *you* plan to live to be ninety if you stuff your body with garbage?" For such a successful guy, Oliver sure lacked common sense. "I refuse to let you eat sweets for dinner. Renée wouldn't approve, either."

"Renée's idea of home cooking is opening a can of liquid diet drink."

That was true, Brooke conceded, except for the past week. "Not while I'm around. When does your open house end?"

"Five." He checked his watch. "I have to be at a meeting by eight, though."

That left plenty of time to eat. "Get home by six or there'll be consequences."

"What kind?" he teased her as he carried his shaving kit into the bathroom.

"I could short-sheet your bed."

"Diabolical." He didn't sound worried. "Where'd you learn a trick like that?"

"Old family tradition."

Brooke's cousins had played pranks like that during family get-togethers. The memory made her wish she hadn't lost touch with her mother's relatives. They'd gathered around after the car crash that had killed her dad, but soon afterward her grandparents had passed away. Then when Brooke was eight, her mom had married her stepfather, Ralph.

A pillar of strength, Mom had called him. A cold, hard pillar, who'd distanced the three of them from all their relatives and everyone else. Brooke believed he'd done so on purpose. After her mother's death, she'd found no trace of her cousins' addresses or phone numbers anywhere in the house.

In any case, she couldn't imagine playing tricks on Oliver. Despite their bickering, she never lost her respect for his innate dignity.

Or her awareness of the danger if he retaliated by wrestling her to the floor or the couch...or the bed. That kind of contact might arouse sensations neither of them would be prepared to address.

Hold on. What?

Before Brooke could gather her thoughts, Oliver returned from the bathroom and tucked his empty suitcase under the bed. "I'm surprised to hear that you cook. You've never struck me as the domestic type."

"I can cook as well as the next person." She genuinely enjoyed trying new recipes. Moreover, the experience of watching friends relax over her meals gave her deep satisfaction.

"The next person would be me, and I can't cook at all. Are we talking about microwaving frozen dinners or whipping up gourmet specials?"

"I guess you'll find out tonight, won't you?" Brooke challenged.

Oliver's jaw worked, and for a moment Brooke feared he'd refuse. Then he reached for his wallet. "Fine. It's generous of you to offer. At least let me pay for the groceries."

"I invited you!"

"I'm not that leech, Kevin." He handed her a fifty. "Think that'll cover it?"

Fifty bucks? "It's way too much."

"Then pick up some breakfast stuff, too, while you're at the store, if you don't mind. I like frozen waffles and syrup."

Breakfast with Oliver. Brooke pictured him lounging in pajamas, his dark hair rumpled and his cheeks scratchy with a morning beard. Eating… What kind of crap?

"Whole-grain cereal and milk," she corrected. "If you aren't careful, you'll develop diabetes and osteoporosis."

"Why should I worry? I might I get hit by a truck first," he shot back, using her own attitude against her.

How annoying! "Oh, go do something useful."

"Exactly my plan. See you." With a nod, he strode out, leaving Brooke steaming.

Being around Oliver made her a little crazy. Thank goodness he was only staying for two days.

Now, what tempting dishes was she going to fix for supper?

Chapter Three

Dinner was far better than Oliver had expected. Spaghetti with pesto, a salad loaded with artichoke hearts and feta cheese, plus some outstanding garlic bread. Which, as Brooke admitted, wasn't healthful at all.

"You have to indulge once in a while," she conceded.

Oliver studied her across Renée's old-fashioned kitchen table. In the glow of the etched-glass chandelier, Brooke's skin glowed. She was pretty, in a girl-next-door way. Although that type had never appealed to Oliver, he could understand why heads turned when she walked into the sandwich shop. "You're full of contradictions."

"If that means I'm unpredictable, great."

"You're that, all right. For instance, this dinner proves to me that you're more organized than you look," he said. "That tells me you could plan for your financial future, if you put your mind to it."

Oliver hated to see Brooke—or anyone—career from one paycheck to the next without an investment plan. With his clients, he saw what a huge difference a smidgen of forethought played in providing economic security.

"In case you missed it, I don't have much of a financial

present, so how could I have a financial future?" Brooke began unwrapping a loaf of something that smelled of cinnamon but looked rather unappealing.

"What's that?" he asked.

"Zucchini bread. For dessert."

"Save it. There'll be dessert at the event I'm attending."

"I won't be there," she reminded him.

That gave Oliver an idea. A bad idea. The scary part was that the more he thought about it, the more feasible it seemed.

Brooke couldn't begin to make the kind of investment Oliver had in mind for himself. However, she could benefit from learning more about how people accumulated wealth. "Come with me."

She cut a slice of the rich, dark bread. "I don't know. Is it a party?"

"Why is Miss Spontaneous giving me the third degree?" he shot back. "Go with the flow."

Her green eyes fixed on him. "I'll bet it's going to be boring. You just want me along to say stupid things and make you laugh."

Her impish response stirred a smile. To Oliver's surprise, he realized he likely would enjoy having her around. Still, honesty required that he explain. "I admit, this will be good for you. And *not* boring." Before she could say no, he added, "You figure I grew up rich, don't you?"

"Actually, I don't spend a lot of time thinking about you. Or how you grew up." She nibbled on the zucchini bread. Nice mouth, Oliver thought. Full lips and teeth just crooked enough to be charming. He wondered what her boss, the orthodontist, thought of them.

Tear those thoughts away. Focus.

"My dad works in a warehouse and I waited tables to pay for community college," he said.

She gave him a grudging nod of respect. "You've done great, then. You must earn a lot."

His energy kicked into high gear, as if he was selling something. Maybe he *was* selling something—an idea. "It isn't just a matter of income. I watch for investment opportunities. That's how I came to own three properties."

Brooke fidgeted. "If you have to be somewhere at eight, we'd better start clearing the table."

"No problem." Scraping back his chair, Oliver carried a stack of dishes to the counter. While Brooke put away food and Oliver loaded the dishwasher, he explained how he'd attended seminars and read books on investing.

"I get it," she conceded. "You're smart."

"Anyone can learn to do this. Including you." He scrubbed residue from the inside of the pasta pot. "Let me show you where I'm headed next."

"You aren't satisfied with what you've got?"

"My goal is to leverage my net worth into millions."

Brooke blew out a long breath. "Wow."

"Tonight, one of my clients, Winston Grooms III, is giving a presentation on a resort he's building in the Caribbean. I thought I'd missed my chance, because it was fully funded, but now they've decided to expand."

Brooke regarded him with interest. "I read about that guy in the paper. Aren't he and his fiancée planning to demolish the cottage down the street?"

"That's them."

With a loud pop, she sealed the lid on a plastic container of leftovers. "That ought to be intriguing. Is she going to be there?"

"You can count on Sherry LaSalle to stick by her man. Like glue." Since being dumped by her first, much older and very wealthy husband, the young socialite had thrown her influence, wealth and heart at the handsome financier.

Brooke washed and dried her hands. "Just let me go change."

"Great!" He'd won. Or, at least, her curiosity about Winston and Sherry had done the trick. "By the way, thanks for dinner."

She flashed him a grin before vanishing into the hallway. How adorable, he thought, and went to tame his end-of-day beard with a razor.

OLIVER'S CAR drove like a dream. Relaxing beside him in the passenger seat, Brooke appreciated the way it glided over the road. Butter-soft cushions, state-of-the-art computer system… He hadn't stinted on *this* investment.

Investments. Ouch. Despite Oliver's assurances, this whole thinking-ahead business made Brooke feel somewhat dizzy. She still didn't understand how you could plan when you were barely hanging on to a job with your fingernails.

Speaking of which, she should have applied a new coat of Slay Me Red to those, because the polish was chipping and she hated to make a bad impression on Oliver's acquaintances. Most notably the glamorous Sherry LaSalle. The newspaper covered her every public appearance.

It focused on her scandalous background, too. An heiress, daughter of a beauty queen and a wealthy entrepreneur, she'd been orphaned at nineteen and had soon fallen in love with a much older attorney. But seven years later he'd dumped Sherry for an even younger woman.

She wore designer dresses and hobnobbed with movie stars. The prospect of joining such sophisticated company for a few hours excited Brooke. She hoped she wouldn't look *too* out of place in her best skirt and sweater. For self-confidence she'd put on her favorite necklace, a gold locket set with a tiny diamond that had been a thirteenth-birthday gift from her mother.

"Where are we going, exactly?" She pictured a fancy hotel, perhaps one of the plush establishments along the coast.

"The Brea Community Center." He paused for a traffic light.

How odd. "We don't have to ride on stationary bicycles while we listen to the talk, do we?" She'd accompanied Renée to the center's fitness rooms once. Her friend had spent an hour working out while Brooke poked along on a treadmill and daydreamed.

"The exercise area has nothing to do with the meeting rooms." He snapped his fingers. "That reminds me. I should post an ad on their notice board."

"For what?"

"A roommate." The car eased forward with the traffic, heading toward downtown Brea. "I've got an ad starting in the paper tomorrow and of course there's my office bulletin board, but I'm in a hurry."

"Why do you want a roommate?" she asked, puzzled.

He braked as an SUV cut in front of them. "I don't."

"Then why are you advertising for one?"

Oliver jerked his head toward the left side of the road, in the general direction of his burned-down condo. "The insurance may cover rebuilding, but I still have to pay the mortgage. I'm losing income on my rental property for as long as a year. Right when I need as much capital as possible to invest."

He must be awfully serious about tonight's presentation to consider sharing space with a stranger. "You picked a bad time to break up with Renée. Otherwise you could have moved in with her."

Oliver shifted into a turn lane. "I prefer being master of my own house."

The pompous statement tickled Brooke. "Ooh. I love that word, *master.*"

The unexpected heat in his glance rippled through her. "Are you flirting with me?"

"With you? No way!" What an outrageous thought.

"Just checking."

She could have sworn he'd responded with interest. Must be a trick of the light from a passing streetlamp.

Oliver went for gorgeous women like Renée. As for Brooke, she wasn't sure what her type was, except...*not* him.

"When you say roommate, do you mean male, female, or doesn't matter?" she asked as they swung onto Birch Street.

"Why should you care?"

"Because I enjoy sticking my nose into other people's business," she responded. "You should have figured that out by now."

"Actually, I have." He chuckled.

Brooke refused to take the bait. "Well?"

"Males only," Oliver said. "Women introduce too many complications."

She had to agree, since it was hard to imagine a female roommate not being attracted to such a sexy guy. On the other hand, males could be tricky, too. "Considering how busy you are, I'd be glad to help you screen candidates."

"Excuse me?"

"You're offering to teach me about investing, so I owe you a favor in return. Besides, I have a lot of intuition."

"You're touting your great insights into character?" Oliver scoffed. "No offense, but in case you've forgotten, your last roomie stiffed you for the rent."

"That's different. He was my boyfriend."

"And this reflects well on your judgment…how?"

She hated to admit he'd hit the bull's-eye. "Look, I chose Kevin with my emotions, not my brain."

"And I'll choose my roommate with *my* brain, too," Oliver responded. "While I appreciate your good intentions, Brooke, I'd rather trust his credit report and a recommendation from his previous landlord."

Irked, she held her tongue. How perverse of Oliver to refuse to let her snoop.

They arrived at the buff-colored, one-story community center, which was located half a block from the Brea Mall. If things got too dull, Brooke supposed she could duck out and go window-shopping.

Then she spotted the picketers.

A rugged-looking guy in blue mechanics' overalls waved a sign that read Go Home Mansion Builders! Save the cottage! proclaimed a placard in the hands of a thirty-ish woman wearing a yellow jogging suit. Half a dozen other signs read Respect Our History! or, more pugnaciously, Harmony Circle: Love It or Leave It. Standing about the entry plaza, the protesters left plenty of space for the well-dressed people heading inside.

"Some people believe that owning a house gives them

the right to call the shots with their neighbors," Oliver grumbled as he slid the sedan into a parking space.

"But I don't see why they bought that old place if they don't like it." The cozy Craftsman-style bungalow and its twin cottage next door gave Brooke a nostalgic feeling whenever she passed them.

"Because it has a double lot, it's in an excellent school district and they like the neighborhood." Twisting around, Oliver fetched a printed sheet from the rear seat. The scent of his aftershave drifted to Brooke.

"So they're going to tear the place down and put up an eyesore," she summarized.

He opened the driver's door. "It's going to be a show-place, and furthermore it conforms to city zoning regulations. Anyone who sees the plans ought to recognize that it'll increase property values, not diminish them."

Brooke hopped out. "Then why aren't there picketers supporting the project?"

Across the car roof, he pinned her with a stare. "You missed your calling. You should have been a lawyer."

"Why?"

"Because you can find a way to argue about everything!"

"I have opinions, that's all." A lawyer, huh? Brooke might have enjoyed that, except for the part about memorizing endless laws and spending years in school.

They crossed the pavement heading toward the picketers. As they approached, the dark-haired fellow in the blue overalls addressed Oliver. "Come to watch Winston and Sherry run roughshod over the rest of us?"

Instead of the polite response Brooke had expected, Oliver snapped, "Blow it out your ear, Rafe."

Brooke couldn't believe he'd uttered such an unprofessional remark. She hoped the picketer wouldn't do something rash, like take a swing at Oliver with his sign.

Instead, the man appeared unruffled—or rather, no more ruffled than before. "If you weren't their agent, you'd be screaming as loud as the rest of us."

"If you didn't live across the street from them, you wouldn't give a damn," Oliver growled.

"Break it up, boys," said the woman in the jogging suit. To Brooke, she said, "I'm Jane McKay. Haven't I seen you with Renée?"

"I'm staying at her house till next weekend. I'm Brooke Bernard." She liked this woman, with her open manner and rumpled brown hair.

Jane indicated Oliver and Rafe, who were exchanging glares. "There's no quarrel like a family quarrel."

"What do you mean?"

"They're cousins."

"That explains a lot." The men did bear a resemblance. Both were dark-haired, although Oliver had blue eyes, instead of brown, and stood a couple of inches taller.

"We're nothing alike," he said without taking his eyes from his opponent.

"You got that right," Rafe growled. "I'm a mere auto mechanic and he's the high priest of money worshipers."

"You own your garage, which makes you as much a capitalist as I am," Oliver shot back. "You of all people should respect others' property rights."

Clearly this pair had a longstanding quarrel going. Brooke sensed an underlying bond, all the same.

"Tempers sure run high over this issue," she said to Jane.

"I try to be objective, but it's really going to hurt to see a piece of history torn down," the woman said. "How sad that Sherry and Winston want to live in Harmony Circle so that their future children can benefit from the family atmosphere and yet they're intent on stirring up animosity."

"And building a monstrosity that's completely out of character with their surroundings," Rafe emphasized.

"However, I *don't* blame Oliver," Jane said. "He had an obligation to sell the property for the owner's estate after she died. Her sister, Minnie, who lives in the other cottage, had to accept the best offer on behalf of the other heirs, so I don't blame her, either. Also," she added, "my house is next door to Oliver's house, and I prefer to remain on good terms with my neighbors."

"Nobody takes this personally except Rafe." Casting a final glare at his cousin, Oliver added, "We don't want to be late for the presentation."

"Guess not." Brooke hoped, as she trailed him inside, that the picketers didn't think she was taking sides. She had no desire to involve herself in a controversy.

She'd forgotten about the bulletin board until Oliver stopped to post a handwritten message seeking a roommate. Then they continued down the wide hallway. Although the fitness center was closed on Sunday evening, several small meeting rooms were in use. With interest she read a placard identifying a class in English as a Second Language and another for a cooking class.

At the end of the hall, they entered a large room set up with folding chairs and a projection screen. She estimated the crowd at about a hundred people, most of whom were leafing through glossy brochures or helping themselves to desserts arrayed along a side table. Prosperous-looking people, Brooke noted, feeling self-conscious about her modest outfit.

To add to her discomfort, her waistband felt just a bit tight. She decided to pass up dessert.

A group had formed around two people who were familiar from newspaper photos. The tall blond man with an air of authority couldn't be anyone other than Winston Grooms III. At his side stood a chic, petite blonde in designer slacks and a silk blouse.

Sherry looked younger than Brooke had expected, and under other circumstances she might have considered trying to strike up a conversation. But perhaps she should, anyway. The woman's oodles of money and the kind of platinum sex appeal that robbed men of their judgment didn't mean she might not enjoy making new friends.

Then a woman at the dessert table swung around and fixed a venomous gaze on Brooke. Good heavens, what was her boss's wife doing here?

And why was she pointing a finger at her and calling everyone's attention to the new arrivals?

"You!" Helen Salonica declared in a voice brassy enough to carry to the farthest corner of the room. "You husband-stealing little tramp!"

Brooke took a step backward and bumped into Oliver. What on earth had provoked such an attack? Any hope of keeping the dispute private vanished when Sherry moved to Helen's side as if closing ranks.

This couldn't be happening. The misguided accusations

had spread to involve the very people Oliver hoped to impress.

Brooke had the miserable feeling she'd just thrown a monkey wrench into his investment plans. It was bad enough to screw up her own life. She'd certainly never intended to damage his.

Chapter Four

What on earth were these women carrying on about? While Oliver didn't want to be sexist, he couldn't imagine a man calling out another guy over some personal quarrel during a business presentation.

At a bar, maybe. Or on the sidewalk outside, when a guy's cousin acted like a wild-eyed radical know-it-all. But not in here.

"Well, well," he murmured to Brooke, trying to break the tension with humor. "It appears I've brought a scarlet woman."

"I'm so sorry." She sounded distraught.

"You're not the one creating a scene," he assured her.

Across the room Winston Grooms raised an eyebrow, as if to say he shared the same bemused reaction. Sherry LaSalle, on the other hand, was glaring daggers at Brooke on behalf of her friend.

"You think I'd allow an upstart like you to destroy my marriage?" The tallish woman with upswept hair advanced on them, with Sherry close behind.

"I work for your husband. That's all," Brooke declared.

"Liar! He bought you that necklace!" Helen Salonica

snapped in a voice sharp enough to draw blood. "I found the receipt in his pants pocket yesterday. Gold chain and locket with a diamond chip!"

"My mother gave me this." Brooke held her ground, a small, brave figure. Of course, she couldn't retreat without steering herself around Oliver.

"This would be the mother who just died?" her tormentor sneered.

Brooke coughed. What was *that* about? Oliver wondered. "I only had one mother," came the indignant response. "She gave me this as a birthday gift. I've worn it for years."

Mrs. Salonica reached out angrily. "Give it here. The money that paid for it is half mine. In fact, I'll take that cheater for everything he's got, starting with this!"

Brooke ducked beneath Oliver's arm. "Are you on drugs, lady?"

Not to be dissuaded, the vengeful woman snatched at her again. Oliver blocked her. "Leave her alone. Do you realize you could be charged with assault for your behavior?"

"Who the hell are you?" she demanded.

Even Sherry LaSalle seemed taken aback by her friend's ferocity. "Oliver Armstrong is our real-estate broker," she said. "Helen, please calm down."

"You're telling me you wouldn't do the same to the witch that stole *your* husband?" Helen Salonica demanded.

Color infused Sherry's face at the reference. "I try to put that behind me."

"Well, I lack your generous spirit. This girl has the audacity to flaunt her ill-gotten loot in front of my friends, and I refuse to allow it."

Oliver spread his arms to fend off another attempted grab. "Brooke's telling the truth. I've seen her wear this locket before." He'd noticed her toying with it on several occasions over the months he'd known her.

"Let me see!" the woman insisted.

"I'm not letting you touch it," Brooke said firmly.

"May I?" Sherry LaSalle held out her hand. "I'd be happy to check for signs of wear. And I promise to give it back to you."

"Even if it's brand-new?" Helen challenged.

"We don't have the right to confiscate anyone's property."

When the other woman settled down, Brooke unhooked the necklace. By the light of Oliver's pen flashlight, Sherry bent down for a closer look.

A small crowd gathered around them. Nothing fascinated people like a domestic drama, Oliver mused.

Dr. Salonica, a heavyset man with thinning hair, chose that moment to meander into the room. Whether he'd been visiting the restroom or he'd just arrived in a separate car, his timing was impeccable. "What's going on?" he asked, approaching the group surrounding his wife.

"I caught you," Helen said triumphantly. "You bought this necklace for your girlfriend, didn't you?"

The orthodontist's face darkened. "Don't be ridiculous."

"You charged a locket with a diamond chip, and here it is."

Sherry clicked off the light. "Not unless the jeweler sold him a locket covered with scratch marks. Sorry, Helen. This isn't new."

The tall woman froze with her head held high. Her husband delivered the final blow.

"You asked me to pick out a birthday present for Lani," Nicholas Salonica told his wife irritably. To the others, he explained, "Wednesday is our daughter's fifteenth birthday."

"You bought the necklace for her?" his wife asked in disbelief.

"I just said so."

"Where is it?" she pressed.

"In the top drawer of your bureau. I mentioned it to you, but you seem to have developed selective hearing." The orthodontist spread his hands apologetically, addressing Sherry and Oliver, rather than Brooke. "All a misunderstanding."

A short distance away, Winston tapped the microphone. "I think everyone's here, so why don't we begin?"

"Good idea. We've had enough excitement for one evening," someone commented, and a chuckle ran through the crowd.

Helen retreated alongside her husband, looking indignant. Too bad they didn't trust each other, Oliver reflected. Why did people bother getting married if they weren't committed to making the relationship work?

As a realtor he had handled numerous home sales resulting from divorces, and as far as he could see nobody profited much except the lawyers. If he ever walked down the aisle he'd... Well, he wasn't sure how he'd act, since he couldn't imagine falling that much in love.

"Did you mean that?" Brooke whispered from her seat beside him. "You remembered me wearing this?"

"I'm not blind." In fact, when he'd bought a Valentine's Day bracelet for Renée, he'd spotted a pair of earrings that would have looked great with the locket. He'd considered sending word to Kevin, but then decided not to waste his time. The guy was too much of a cheapskate to spring for them.

The lights dimmed. On the screen there appeared an architect's rendering in vivid tropical colors. Scene after scene brought to life a world-class resort about to be built on the Caribbean island of Santa Martina. Luxury suites, convention facilities, a golf course, two helipads, a private harbor—and the latest addition to the plans, a clinic where guests could receive beauty treatments and undergo plastic surgery.

"It's brilliant," Oliver whispered.

"One-stop shopping," Brooke murmured.

"We're already receiving bookings from tour agencies in Japan, Argentina and other countries," Winston continued. "The original block of rooms is sold out for the first year and a half after the projected opening."

Oliver could almost taste the excitement. In addition to investing, he longed to play a more significant role in the project. Was there a chance Winston might be willing to involve him in the marketing end?

The financier ran over the project timeline, then moved on to the closing. "Because we only have a few opportunities left, we're asking participants for a minimum investment of one million dollars each."

A million dollars?

Oliver felt as if he'd been sucker punched. Thinking about how to raise a quarter of that—which had been the buy-in amount the first time around—he'd crunched numbers until his brain had whirled. Paradise was now officially out of his league.

Deflated, he sank back. Several other audience members appeared to be disappointed, as well, but not all of them. Helen Salonica was poking her husband in the ribs, and if Oliver read her lip movements correctly she was whispering, "Let's do it."

Where did an orthodontist get that kind of money? Must be a lot of kids in Brea with crooked teeth.

In a fog, Oliver listened to a series of questions and answers from the floor. No point in asking if Winston might accept a lesser sum. Too humiliating, and besides, Oliver wasn't even close to the minimum.

Brooke remained quiet until they were back in the car. "Too high, huh?"

His throat tight, Oliver nodded. All the same he appreciated her sensitivity.

She fingered her locket. "There'll be other developments, right?"

"No doubt." *But not like this.* There in the audience he had recognized several billionaires and a number of CEOs. Those were the people who associated with Sherry LaSalle and Winston Grooms III. A mere real-estate broker didn't often get invited into such company, and he doubted he'd be so lucky again for a long while.

This had been, he'd imagined, his breakthrough opportunity. Now it was gone.

Still, wallowing in disappointment went against Oliver's nature. Nor did he want to impose his bad mood on Brooke. Pulling his thoughts back into a lighter mode, he asked, "What's *your* dream?"

"A week at that resort, some sunning on the beach and then getting my nails and hair done," she said.

"That's as high as you aspire?"

"A week every year," she amended.

"Get serious." He'd like to hear about her goals, if she had any. Husband and home? Winning the lottery? Making it to the finals on *American Idol?*

"I wouldn't mind having a cottage like the one Sherry and Winston are so eager to knock down," she admitted. "Why can't they be happy there?"

"I doubt that woman has ever lived in a house smaller than five thousand square feet," he remarked.

"How big's the cottage? I have no idea."

Having handled the sale, he could tell her. "Nine hundred and fifty."

"Sounds big to me. Bigger than my last apartment, anyway." Brooke gazed out at the passing lights. "There's a woman who leads a charmed life—not that I'm envious. Somebody *did* steal her husband, after all."

Much as Oliver respected Sherry, he didn't believe in overlooking obvious faults. "What goes around comes around."

"What's that mean?"

"Sherry wasn't Elliott LaSalle's first wife, you know," he explained.

Her eyes widened. "She wasn't?"

"He's got two kids almost as old as she is. In fact, one of them's older than his latest squeeze. But that's irrelevant."

"Tell all! I love gossip."

"You don't love it so much when you're the brunt of it."

Brooke shrugged. "Okay, so I'm two-faced. Now, tell me what happened to wife number one."

"You're aware that Elliott was the attorney who handled her parents' estate? Well, he gave her a shoulder to cry on, dumped his wife and whisked Little Miss Sunshine to the altar."

To Oliver's way of thinking, the guy had abused a position

of trust. As a beautiful, vulnerable nineteen-year-old heiress, Sherry must have made an appealing target. Of course, that didn't excuse her decision to take up with a married man.

Brooke planted her bare feet on the dashboard. "I was wondering why a man would drop a wife as gorgeous as she is. From what you say, it sounds as if this Elliott person is kind of predatory."

"Good word," he agreed.

"Poor Sherry."

"You feel sorry for her?" Oliver would have expected envy or resentment, in light of Sherry's wealth compared to Brooke's ongoing struggle to make ends meet.

"She seems like a nice person. Although that doesn't explain why she's friends with Helen Salonica." Brooke's nose wrinkled. "I wish I had a better opinion of that woman, but she's so nasty."

"You held up pretty well against her tonight," he said.

"I just hope she doesn't get me fired."

"She can't fire you. That's up to your boss, isn't it?" Oliver presumed that Mrs. Salonica played no role in running the office.

"True. Let's just say she has influence."

"Well, *he* has a responsibility to treat his employees well." If Nicholas Salonica punished Brooke for his decision to keep his buddy Kevin's secrets, Oliver would have a few choice words to say to the man. The fact that the orthodontist wasn't a potential client—his brother owned a rival real-estate brokerage—didn't figure into the matter. Much.

Pulling into Renée's driveway, he observed, "We're home."

"That sounds nice," Brooke admitted. "Even if neither of us actually lives here."

"For tonight, we do."

"Anyplace I hang my sunglasses is home," she conceded.

Going inside with her felt comfortable. Usually Oliver preferred collecting his thoughts in silence, but Brooke's humming served as the most pleasant kind of white noise.

Also, her cheerful air had the welcome effect of diverting his thoughts from his disappointment about the resort. After swapping his suit for jeans and a T-shirt, Oliver settled on the couch beside her to watch a science-fiction show on TV. Nice to discover she enjoyed *Star Trek* reruns as much as he did.

Lounging on the sofa, Brooke draped her legs over his lap as if he were part of the furniture. She had slender legs, well shaped, with pretty feet. Although he'd seen those knockout red toenails before, they seemed much sexier stretched across the velour.

Did this woman have any idea what effect the contact was having on him? Her legs rubbed against Oliver whenever she shifted, and at this angle her breasts looked fuller than he remembered. The locket dipped into the cleavage as if inviting him to explore.

Right. She'd slap his face if he tried, and he'd deserve it.

Oliver stifled a groan. How fortunate that Renée was returning tomorrow to serve as a buffer.

The notion startled him. Renée, a buffer? He'd never given Brooke a moment's thought when he was dating her more glamorous friend. Today's proximity must be having an odd effect on his libido.

Temporary insanity. It would disappear soon enough, he had no doubt.

FOR BROOKE, Monday passed with surprising smoothness. Surprising, because for the first time in weeks no disasters struck.

Helen Salonica stayed away from her husband's office; Dr. Salonica treated the staff to a new coffeemaker; and Renée returned from Las Vegas in high spirits, having won a small sum at blackjack.

Best of all, Oliver slept on the couch that night. Of course, Brooke wouldn't have objected to his renewing the relationship with Renée, but she'd hate to see them sleep together and regret it afterward.

There wasn't much danger of that, however, because Renée had a date Monday evening. She didn't say whom she was meeting and, anyway, Oliver was out until late with clients.

Brooke ate microwaved popcorn and watched old episodes of *Desperate Housewives* from her hostess's DVD collection. Later, she helped Oliver make up the couch, brushing aside popcorn kernels as they put on the set of sheets.

She hoped Oliver wouldn't notice the quivers of response that ran through her when they brushed against each other. The guy *was* easy on the eyes, as well as fun to be around. And something more. He really listened to her and seemed to care whether she picked up the pieces of her life.

A good friend. And occasionally a pain in the neck. On Tuesday morning she staggered into the kitchen, barely awake, to discover that he'd arranged some of her gaudier sunglasses on various appliances so there appeared to be an audience watching them eat breakfast.

Brooke pretended not to notice. Renée appeared to be stifling giggles.

After finishing his toast, Oliver left his belongings with a promise to pick them up after work. And that, Brooke reflected, might just be the last time she'd say more than a passing hello to him for, well, eternity.

Too bad. She'd enjoyed the playful verbal sparring. Even if she didn't appreciate having to put away the sunglasses after he left.

The rest of Tuesday went downhill from there, however.

Soon after the office opened, Helen Salonica arrived and confronted her husband in his private office. Their voices carried—okay, Brooke had to cup her ears, but they were more or less loud enough to reach the front desk.

"Why did you leave the house in such a rush?" the orthodontist's wife demanded in her shrill soprano. "We didn't finish our discussion, and I want to get this show on the road before the resort's fully funded."

"We *did* finish, as far as I'm concerned, and I have a patient waiting in the chair," he snapped back. "We've been hashing this out since Sunday. We do not have a million dollars to throw around, and that's that."

"Our net worth is well above that. Why leave it sitting around, when we could be earning a bundle? It's ridiculous!"

"Our money is invested in our house and this business. I'm not leaping into some scheme just to impress your snooty friend."

"At least let our accountant figure out how much we could raise. I'll bet it's easier than you think. For instance, if you look at the kids' college fund—"

"Are you crazy? We're not touching that."

Someone closed an inner door. Judging by Helen

Salonica's smug expression when she emerged, however, she must have prevailed.

Then she caught sight of Brooke. Tight-jawed, the woman approached the counter and growled, "Don't think you're putting anything over on me, you little schemer. I may have been wrong about the necklace, but you're up to something. If I were you, I'd start looking for another job."

Faye, who hated dustups of any sort, got busy on the phone, calling to remind patients about scheduled visits.

"I'm not up to anything, Mrs. Salonica," Brooke replied. "I'm sorry if you don't feel you can trust your husband, but that isn't because of me."

"Oh, the whole world knows you're Miss Innocent."

Brooke wasn't sure how to respond. Innocent? Well, hardly. Considering how much her stomach had been bothering her in the mornings, she wished she still *was* a virgin.

Her boss's wife appeared to expect a response, so she said, "Please accept my word that I have nothing to do with any problems in your marriage."

"As if your word means anything. And we aren't having problems!" With a sniff of disdain, the woman turned and brushed past a young girl who was just signing in.

Faye hung up, waited until the girl rejoined her mother in the waiting area and said to Brooke, "You shouldn't provoke her."

"I don't. Not on purpose."

"It's almost as if you like being in the middle of a tornado." The other receptionist twisted a lock of stringy hair around her finger.

"Isn't the eye of the storm supposed to be peaceful?" Brooke asked.

"That's hurricanes, not tornadoes."

How absurd to be discussing weather phenomena in an orthodontist's office. Faye seemed serious about the whole business, too. Hoping to lighten the mood of her roommate-to-be, Brooke said, "Okay, but a tornado carried Dorothy to Oz."

"So?"

"Wouldn't you like to visit the Emerald City?"

"Don't be ridiculous. That's fiction."

Both phone lines rang, ending the discussion. Brooke made a mental note to avoid teasing Faye. Literal-minded people fell short when it came to exchanging verbal volleys.

Oliver would have responded to her comments with some crack about flying monkeys and wicked witches. Brooke missed him already.

At lunchtime, she met Renée at the sandwich shop. Despite sharing living quarters, they still hadn't had a chance to catch up on the weekend's activities, and Brooke listened with delight as her friend recounted her adventures in Las Vegas.

Willowy and blond, with a heart-stopping face, Renée attracted men as naturally as Brooke attracted trouble, yet she seemed utterly free of vanity. She described being plied with drinks—which had no evident effect on her, while various men had slid under the table—and enjoying a performance of Cirque du Soleil at a casino theater.

Questioned about *her* weekend, Brooke described the evening encounter with Helen and Sherry. "Mrs. LaSalle seems like she might be a nice person, even if she *is* rich."

"The two qualities aren't mutually exclusive," Renée observed.

Brooke downed a bite of her avocado-and-crab sandwich before saying, "Yeah, but people that wealthy live in a different dimension."

"I suppose in some ways they do," Renée agreed. "Speaking of dimensions, have you taken that pregnancy test yet?"

Oops. Brooke should have anticipated the question. "Not with Oliver in the house."

"He wasn't home most of last night, was he?"

"I'm not pregnant," Brooke told her. "I can't be."

A gasp from alongside drew her attention to Faye, who must have been padding by at that inopportune moment. "You're pregnant?"

"No." Brooke peered around to see who else had heard. She didn't recognize any of the other nearby diners.

"That settles it, Brooke!" Faye said. "You are not moving in with us."

"What?" Brooke couldn't believe the woman's illogical decision. Or her unfairness. "Even if I were pregnant, I'm not planning on raising a baby in your apartment."

"Oh? What are you planning to do with it?"

"There *is* no baby!" Probably.

Renée intervened. "It's not fair to leave Brooke with nowhere to go on such short notice. If she does turn out to be expecting, I'm sure she'll find another place before she delivers."

Faye's thin face registered a whole series of emotions, none of them sympathy. "I was having second thoughts, anyway—she's just plain trouble! Can you imagine if Mrs. Salonica lumps us together? We could both lose our jobs."

"That's quite a leap," Brooke told her.

"It's not my fault you're so…so…ebullient."

"*Ebullient* means *cheerful*," Renée remarked.

"It means…like…a bull in a china shop!" Faye burst out. "And she is. There's constant turmoil in the office because of her."

Although the occasional outburst from Helen Salonica didn't amount to constant turmoil, Brooke couldn't force the other receptionist to let her move in. She hadn't signed a lease, and in any case, what an uncomfortable situation it was. Besides, she hadn't been thrilled about the prospect of living with her fussbudget coworker. "Don't worry. I'm not going to impose on someone who doesn't want me."

"Good. I'm sure you'll find another place." Her nose twitching like a mouse who'd just spotted a cat, Faye hustled out of the sandwich shop.

Renée followed her departure with dismay. "Oh, dear. I can't postpone my remodeling."

"I don't expect you to. Something will turn up for me." Still musing about her situation, Brooke added, "I'm glad I don't have to go through life afraid of my shadow like Faye."

"So you aren't afraid of anything, are you?" Renée challenged. "I could name one thing that scares the heck out of you."

"What?"

"Use the kit, Brooke. If you're pregnant, Kevin owes you support. And back rent. Either way, you need to find out."

"I'm *not* afraid. But the whole idea of Kevin having to pay me… It doesn't seem right."

Renée's expression swung from doubt to incredulity. "Don't tell me you feel sorry for the jerk!"

"Not for him, for his kids," Brooke explained. "I've felt guilty ever since I learned about his daughters. And since I figured out that the separation wasn't his wife's choice. They deserve better than to have him supporting me and a child."

"You believe a weasel like Kevin is suddenly going to become a decent husband and father?"

"If you thought he was a weasel, you should have told me."

"I wasn't sure until it was too late," Renée conceded. "Now, about that test…"

Brooke sighed. "Sooner or later. In the meantime, I've got a good idea."

"What's that?"

Brooke paused as a couple of real-estate agents she recognized strolled past. She didn't want Oliver's associates overhearing any part of this conversation.

When they reached the takeout counter, she continued in a low voice, "I'll move in with Oliver. He needs a roommate. That would solve my immediate problem, and his, too."

"You think he'll agree?"

"The worst he can say is no." Or he could laugh uproariously. Which would be pretty humiliating.

Her friend shook her head. "You're a grown-up and so's he. But if you want my opinion…" Renée broke off. "Forget my opinion. Maybe you *won't* kill each other."

That didn't sound like a blessing. Nevertheless, Brooke considered this an excellent solution to her problems.

The only challenge remaining would be to persuade Oliver. And she was already formulating a plan for how to handle *that*.

Chapter Five

"What gives?" Oliver stared grumpily at the meal Brooke had prepared, acknowledging that it smelled delicious. Baked chicken, saffron rice and a vegetable. For heaven's sake, he hadn't mentioned eating supper at Renée's, even though this *was* his last evening.

He'd packed his bags. Although it was already dark outside, he might as well move. His house had aired out, and when he'd driven by earlier the exterminator had been removing the Keep Out signs.

"It's a farewell dinner." Brooke regarded him optimistically.

He didn't mean to take out his crankiness on her—or on their hostess, who stood at the sink opening a diet shake and watching them both. He noted that *she* didn't intend to eat.

He'd had a rough afternoon, highlighted by a meeting of fellow condominium owners to discuss rebuilding. Trying to get them to agree on anything was like herding wildcats. Rabid wildcats. Why weren't they as eager to replace their lost homes as he was? Instead of cooperating, they'd squabbled over improvements, with one man holding out for solar panels that their insurance didn't cover.

The dispute had dampened Oliver's appetite, and the prospect of a sit-down meal rubbed him the wrong way. He looked for a detail to criticize. "I hate brussels sprouts."

"Those aren't brussels sprouts. They're baby cabbages." Brooke defended her vegetables like a mother guarding her offspring.

"Same thing."

"You're being obstinate," she declared.

"I was born obstinate."

"People can change."

At the sink, Renée's head swiveled back and forth, as if she were following a tennis match.

"I don't wish to change," Oliver retorted. "Sit-down meals waste time. I'd rather eat on the run."

"See here, young man, you'll ruin your health!"

Although he was tempted to laugh at her impudence, that would be a mistake, because then he might yield. If he ate any more of her cooking, the minx might be encouraged to start dropping by his office with muffins and other goodies.

He couldn't recall a time before college when he hadn't been overweight. Whenever his father lost his temper, which happened often, his mom had gone on a cooking jag. His big brother, Bill, used to shed calories on the football field, while his kid sister, Melanie, had burned them off hopping up and down to wait on their father. Shy and sensitive, Oliver had eaten to keep the peace and had suffered taunts and rejection at school as a result.

Once he began working his way through community college, however, he'd lacked both money and free time. Fast-food specials had filled the bill. Contrary to popular opinion, he'd lost rather than gained weight because he ate solely when he was hungry.

To this day Oliver disliked sitting down to meals, not so much because of the weight issue as because of the bad memories.

"Stop pestering the man and make your case, Brooke," Renée advised.

"What case?" he asked.

His impish companion drooped. "I hoped we'd have a chance to chat over dinner. I was trying to put you in a good mood."

"To chat about what?"

She folded her arms. "I can't move in with the other receptionist, after all."

While he sympathized, he failed to see any connection between that piece of news and his mood, pleasant or otherwise. "What happened?"

"She's afraid Helen Salonica will lump us together and have us both fired."

That struck Oliver as somewhat farfetched. However, when he glanced at Renée for confirmation, she nodded.

"So," Brooke continued, "since you're looking for a roommate, I figured I'd apply. Depending on how much the rent is, of course. I'm easy to get along with, as you saw this weekend—right? We even enjoy the same TV shows. And I'm convenient. As in doing the cooking."

Oliver repressed a shudder at the thought of making this arrangement permanent. Nutritious meals on the table every night. Sunglasses-wearing teddy bears hogging all the chairs. Brooke's adorable bare feet on the coffee table. All that coziness invading his personal space.

Sure, he liked her. But intimacy made him hyperventilate.

And if they spent many more evenings curled up together, he might succumb to less-than-admirable instincts.

Sex with Brooke might thrill them both in the short run, but inevitably there'd be complications.

Fortunately he had the perfect excuse.

"I already found a roommate," he said. "Name of Gary Lincoln. He's relocating from Utah and he saw my ad in the paper."

"A total stranger!" she protested. "That means you have no idea what kind of person he is."

Oliver sneaked a last, regretful glance at the delicious food Brooke had made and toted his bags toward the door. "I checked him out. Great credit rating and raves from his landlord in Salt Lake City. He's dropping by the office tomorrow morning to sign a lease, write a check and pick up the key."

"But—"

"It's a done deal, Brooke. Sorry."

She wandered outside in his wake. A twinge of something between guilt and protectiveness stole over Oliver as he regarded her small, forlorn figure.

When she was around, he had to admit, the air crackled with electricity. Maybe she *was* a drama magnet, but it had been fun occupying a front-row seat.

Not on a full-time basis, though. He'd much rather arrive home at the end of the day to find a no-maintenance guy such as Gary Lincoln eating a takeout meal and then disappearing into the den to play videogames. The man appeared to be articulate, smart and problem-free.

Boring. But *good* boring.

"What's in the boxes?" Brooke peered into the back of his car. "Wow! A new TV and digital recorder."

"The insurance company will reimburse me." Oliver rearranged the contents of the trunk to clear space for his bags.

"Did you buy furniture, too?"

"I'm renting the bare minimum until my condo's rebuilt." He closed the trunk and turned to face her. "Brooke, are you that desperate? You must have other friends you can camp with."

"Sure. Don't worry about *me.*" She shrugged, as if to say she already had a backup plan. "Good luck with everything."

"You, too." He felt as if they were saying farewell before a long separation, when in reality they bumped into each other often by their offices. Maybe he should continue to hog spaces in front of Smile Central so she'd storm over and read him the riot act from time to time. "If Helen Salonica goes over the edge, you can call on me for a job recommendation."

"Thanks." She stepped away. "I hope you get your share of that resort or something even better."

With a nod, Oliver swung himself into the car and turned on the ignition. Brushing aside a brief pang of regret, he focused on the anticipation of settling into his new digs.

As a treat he had a bag of chips and some bean dip waiting for him there.

AFTER NIBBLING at the food she'd made and storing the copious leftovers, Brooke planted herself in the living room. Over the next few hours, she phoned and e-mailed all her acquaintances to ask if anyone needed a roommate. Aside from garnering plenty of sympathy, she got nowhere.

Brooke refused to blame Faye or Kevin or anyone else. Negative thinking attracted bad luck. Besides, she had five days left before H day.

As in, Homeless.

On Wednesday, she drove the short distance home for lunch to munch on cold chicken and microwaved brussels sprouts. Since she'd already scanned newspaper ads and the Internet without success, she decided to spend the rest of her break checking out bulletin boards at the community center and other spots in town.

Rounding the curve on Harmony Road, Brooke slowed to let a white cat cross the street. To her left, roses ran riot in the yard of number ten, one of the two cottages that dated back to the 1920s.

The owner of the cottage, Minnie Ortiz, kept the place in beautiful shape, and Brooke took a moment to admire the fresh paint, old-fashioned shutters and willow porch furniture. Next door, number nine, the color had faded on the smaller structure and weeds were sprouting in the yard. It must have been beautiful back in the days when Minnie's sister had lived there, though.

Brooke paid little heed to the expensive sedan parked in front until a slim blond woman rounded the corner of the vintage bungalow. Her attention focused on the view of the nearby hills, she raised her camera for a shot.

Brooke caught her breath. Sherry LaSalle was examining her property. *If I owned a place like this, I'd examine it every chance I got.*

Except, of course, that Sherry wasn't admiring the cottage. Perhaps she was figuring out where she wanted to place the picture windows in the mansion she and Winston planned to build on the site. Well, as Oliver contended, Sherry and Winston had bought the house and they had the legal right to replace it. Still, what a shame for the charming bungalow to stand empty while debate raged over its fate. For one thing, it invited vandalism.

What the owner needed was a house-sitter.

Brooke left her car and sauntered over. Without an entourage, and dressed in jeans and a knit top, Sherry LaSalle seemed more approachable. After all, they were close to the same height and no more than a few years apart in age.

"Beautiful place," Brooke observed.

The other woman turned with a start, her cool air instantly dispelling the illusion of accessibility. "What are *you* doing here? And what are those hideous things you're wearing?"

For today, Brooke had selected an oversize pair of rhinestone-bedecked sunglasses from her collection. "I guess these *are* a little gaudy." She shifted them onto the top of her head. "I was on my way back to work. I'm staying with a girlfriend down the street."

"Who?"

"Renée Trent."

Sherry paused as if processing the information. "I don't think her name's on the list," she mused, perhaps referring to the petition being circulated to preserve the cottage.

"She's not political." Then, judging that response inadequate, Brooke added, "Me, neither."

"Something I can do for you?"

Okay, forget about establishing rapport. Better talk fast, while she had the chance. "Renée's remodeling her house starting next week, and I need a place to stay. I gather nobody's living here, and it occurred to me you might like a house-sitter for security reasons."

Rather than warming up, the divorcée turned positively icy. "I would never betray a friend."

"Neither would I. What's that got to do with anything?"

"When Elliott left me, so did a lot of my friends, or at

least women I considered friends," Sherry said stiffly. "Helen Salonica stuck by me."

Aha. Brooke had to admire her loyalty. But it was so misplaced. "She admits she was wrong about the locket. You examined it."

"Regardless, she's convinced you're after her husband." Sherry's eyes narrowed. "And in my opinion where there's smoke, there's fire."

"I have zero interest in Dr. Salonica, and he's never shown the least bit of interest in me."

"Other than buying you flowers with his personal credit card? Helen says he puts staff expenses on his business account."

That was news to Brooke. "I have no idea how he handles his money and I don't care. I'm sorry his wife is upset. If there was anything I could do to reassure her, I would."

"Glad to hear it." Sherry thrust her camera into a designer handbag that must have cost more than Brooke earned in a month. "Quit your job and find another one."

Brooke stared at her. "Excuse me?"

"That's what an honest person would do."

That's what a spoiled rich woman who's never had to work a day in her life would say. Reining in her temper, Brooke struggled to be diplomatic. "Jobs don't fall into people's laps whenever they want them, and I can't afford to be out of work."

"You could collect unemployment."

"That's if you get laid off. Not if you quit!"

Sherry dismissed the statement. "Everybody needs receptionists. I'm sure you could land another position in no time. *If* you wanted to help save this marriage, which you obviously don't."

Brooke teetered on the verge of outrage. "I understand your loyalty to Helen—"

"She's Mrs. Salonica to you, and you'd better remember it."

The fury in the other woman's tone puzzled Brooke. "Fine. That's no reason to get all worked up. Aside from her mistaken ideas about me, did I do something to tick you off?"

"You have no idea what it's like to have someone steal your husband," Sherry fumed. "I never had a clue about how home wreckers operate until it was too late. I hope Helen makes your life miserable."

From down the block drifted the playful shouts of small children, along with the aroma of grilled cheese sandwiches. Brooke abandoned the notion of living in the cottage and gave vent to her indignation.

"Well, you're a fine one to accuse *me*," she told the other woman. "Everybody knows you stole your husband from his first wife."

Sherry's head jerked as if she'd been slapped. After a stunned moment, she replied, "No, I didn't. They were already estranged."

"Who told you that? Him, I'll bet." The other woman's shock appeared genuine. Perhaps she'd never considered the situation in this light, Brooke thought with a twinge of sympathy. "Hey, some of us can be a little too trusting when it comes to guys."

"You and I are *nothing* alike." The words were ground out viciously. "I would *never* stoop to begging favors. I can't believe you had the nerve to ask me for a free place to live."

"We can't all be heiresses, can we?" Brooke snapped, and marched back to her car before Sherry could reply.

Fuming, she started the engine. She hadn't meant to engage in a quarrel, for heaven's sake. Why did the woman have to be so rude?

On Brooke's left she spotted Oliver's house, a single-story structure with a bay window. Longing arced through her. With a few homey touches, such as flowered curtains instead of blinds, it would be a splendid place to stay. And what fun it would be to kid around with Oliver every day!

She'd lost it all to a newcomer from Utah. Who must be that man in his thirties emerging through the front door with a large box in his arms.

Brooke conducted a quick assessment. Neatly groomed and well dressed, he had a bland face that wouldn't stand out in a crowd. Or on its own, either.

Wait a minute. If the guy was moving in, why was he carrying a box *out* of the house?

And it was labeled with the same brand name of the television she'd glimpsed in Oliver's trunk that morning.

Brooke pulled over to the curb. The fellow, busy maneuvering the heavy box down the steps, didn't appear to notice her sitting there on the far side of the street.

An unmarked white van sat in front of the house, its rear doors open. Those weren't Utah license plates, however—they were from Nevada. Puzzled, Brooke rolled down her window and sank into the seat.

Opening her cell phone, she fumbled in the glove box until she found a promotional pad of Oliver's that she'd been using for scratch paper. It listed his office and—bingo!—his cell number.

She tapped in the number. Opposite her, Mr. Not-from-Utah hoisted the box and pushed it into the van.

After two rings, a familiar voice said, "Oliver Armstrong."

"It's Brooke." She hurried on. "This is weird. That guy you rented to? At least I think it's him… He just carried your TV out of the house and put the box in his van. Which isn't from Utah, it's from Nevada."

"Excuse me, what are you doing there?"

"I was driving by. He caught my attention."

With exaggerated patience, he said, "Brooke, I checked this guy out, like I told you. This morning, he paid me a deposit and a month's rent in advance. Maybe he bought a TV just like mine and decided to return it."

The fellow darted into the house. "Yes, but…" She clutched the phone. "He's just come out with your digital recorder."

"What? Are you sure?"

"Yeah. He's shoving it into his van."

"Describe him."

"Medium coloring, medium height, gray slacks, dark blue V-neck sweater with a light blue shirt."

"That sounds like Gary. Keep an eye on him!" Quickly he added, "Don't take any risks. I'm coming over right now."

Mr. Grabby Hands went back inside. Brooke doubted he'd hang around long enough for Oliver to arrive, though. "Why don't you call the cops?"

"Because that's a lousy thing to do to my new house-mate. He might have a valid explanation."

The man reappeared, his hands full once again. "He's carrying a table lamp with a round yellow base. Is that yours?"

"It's rented. You're right—I'm calling the police. Thanks, Brooke." The phone cut off.

She scrunched low in her seat, determined to keep this

thief in view. At least he didn't appear to pose a threat to anyone.

Then a compact car rolled into the driveway next door. She recognized the woman who emerged as Jane McKay, the neighbor she'd met on the picket line. A straight skirt and tailored blouse flattered her curves a lot better than that jogging suit she'd worn previously.

Having stowed the lamp, Gary Lincoln rushed inside again. His nervous movements must have caught Jane's attention, because she stood there staring after him.

Don't spook him! Brooke didn't fancy the prospect of pursuing a van across town, although she'd do it if she had to.

Out trotted the thief with a suitcase identical to Oliver's. The creep was stealing clothes and toiletries. How low could you stoop?

Brooke ground her teeth as the man half trotted toward his vehicle. Suppose he got away? How awful for Oliver, who'd already lost almost everything in the fire, to be victimized again.

"Excuse me," Jane called. "What are you doing?"

Gary paused on the walkway. "Moving in with Oliver."

Don't challenge him. Cornered rats are the most dangerous kind.

"Oh, you're his new housemate?" Jane's open manner revealed no suspicion. Thank goodness. "I'm Dr. Jane McKay. Nice to meet you." Hand extended, she approached the fellow.

Brooke wanted to shout at her not to touch him. Clearly the man was slime personified. Yet if she leaped out yelling, "Get back!" she'd warn him off before the police could arrive.

Holding her breath, she watched the neighbor stride unsuspectingly toward the crook. Jane—Dr. Jane—appeared to be in a chatty mood. "I came home for lunch. My office is a mile away on Central. What kind of work do you do?"

The man set down the suitcase to shake hands. "Estates and trusts."

As in looting them, no doubt.

"You're an attorney?"

"I work in the legal field, yes." Possibly true, if you considered serving time in prison "working in the legal field."

As they finished shaking hands, Jane glanced down at the suitcase. Her forehead furrowed. "That has Oliver's name tag on it." She looked up in confusion. "Why are you taking that to your van?"

"He, uh, said I could borrow it. To put my stuff in. I have to make another trip." The man hefted the case.

"That doesn't look empty to me," she challenged. "Would you mind opening it?"

"Are you always this pushy?"

She recoiled. "If you think that's going to allay my suspicions, you're very much mistaken."

"I haven't got all day." He started off with the bag.

"Stop right there!" she commanded, storming after him.

Brooke admired the woman's courage. Too bad she didn't exercise more caution.

I'm a fine one to talk. If this was Oliver's thinking when he chided Brooke about her impulsiveness, she began to see his point.

"Mind your own business," the man snapped back as he headed for the rear of the vehicle.

"What else do you have in the van?" Jane's heels

clicked on the sidewalk as she kept pace. "My house got burglarized once, and I won't tolerate that sort of thing!"

Brooke wished she could somehow stop Jane from provoking this guy. A few household goods weren't worth the risk of personal injury.

Too late, however.

The events that followed seemed to occur in extra-crisp high definition, every detail standing out with perfect clarity. Jane's jaw dropped as she glimpsed the contents of the van. And then Gary Lincoln grasped her arm and dragged her toward the van, and horror replaced outrage on her face.

The creep was kidnapping Jane just to shut her up! Brooke's heart shifted into overdrive.

She couldn't wait for help to arrive. She had to do something *now*.

Tossing aside her sunglasses and jumping from her car, she barreled across the street. Lincoln's startled expression barely had a chance to register before Brooke lowered her head and butted full speed into his stomach.

Chapter Six

Brooke felt the air *whoosh* out of the man as her head connected with his midsection. He staggered backward and collapsed on the grass, leaving her stumbling. Only Jane's grip on her arm prevented a spectacular wipeout.

The impact vibrated through Brooke's neck and shoulders until she felt like a giant bell. Any moment, the ringing should begin to fade, she thought as she remained bent over in agony, but instead of fading, it grew louder and more shrill.

Oh, that wasn't reverberation. It was sirens.

A police car pulled up and out stepped two uniformed women. They approached the scene, scanning the situation intently.

On the grass Gary Lincoln gasped for breath, his face having taken on a greenish cast. With an effort, Brooke straightened. Her head swam, but she managed to maintain her balance.

"That man tried to kidnap me," Jane said, pointing a finger in Lincoln's direction. "I caught him robbing my neighbor's house."

The man's face twisted with contempt. "I signed a rental

agreement on this house today. These women must be some kind of vigilante maniacs. That one assaulted me!" He indicated Brooke.

"He was stealing Oliver's stuff," Brooke told the officers as her ears continued to thrum.

"I'll testify to that," Jane said.

"Does anyone need medical attention?" one of the officers asked. When they all declined, her partner asked to see everyone's identification.

A wave of relief swept over Brooke as Oliver's sedan pulled up behind the cruiser. He hurried out clutching a sheaf of papers. "That's the home owner right there."

Everyone turned. "He'll vouch for me," Lincoln announced with a hint of nervousness. "Hey, Armstrong! Tell these people I live here, will you?"

Oliver regarded the man in disgust. "You signed a contract in the name of Gary Lincoln, all right. Too bad you aren't him."

That explained a lot, Brooke thought. So the guy had obtained a key under false pretenses.

After requesting Oliver's ID, one of the officers said, "You're the person who called us."

"Yes, ma'am." He handed her a sheet of paper. "As soon as I got off the phone, I noticed this alert on my computer. The real Gary Lincoln had just notified the credit agencies I contacted that he's the victim of identity theft."

He showed the policewoman a rental agreement and a check. "He forged signatures on both of these."

"We'll need those for evidence."

"Yes, of course." Oliver relinquished them at once.

The man on the lawn seemed to shrink with every word that was spoken. He'd run out of lies, Brooke figured.

There was a lot to be said for researching a guy's background. But that still didn't substitute for trusting your gut reaction.

Maybe Oliver would be more willing to trust Brooke's intuition when it came to choosing his next roommate.

ANSWERING QUESTIONS, identifying the stolen property and walking through the house to assess the situation took more than an hour. The cops were thorough and professional.

After they left with their prisoner in handcuffs, Oliver called Dr. Salonica to explain Brooke's absence and relate how she'd saved the day. "You'll read about it in the paper," he assured the orthodontist. "There's a reporter outside snapping pictures."

He'd been less than thrilled when the woman arrived, fearing her presence might distress the obviously dazed Brooke. Instead, however, the prospect of being featured in the paper had proved a welcome distraction.

Standing on the sidewalk, Oliver watched Brooke and Jane pose atop the porch steps. What a contrast between the pair—Jane tall and angular with short, wispy hair, and Brooke petite, curvy and soft.

"Tell her to take the rest of the day off," Dr. Salonica said. "Be sure to tell the reporter where she works and that we're proud to have a heroine on our staff."

"Good publicity," Oliver noted.

"For you, too. You *did* mention Archway Real Estate, right?"

"Well, yes."

He didn't mean to capitalize on the situation, though. Oliver was just grateful that Brooke had spotted the illicit activity, not so much because of the stolen property but because she'd been there to save Jane.

They both owed Brooke a huge debt.

Which could be repaid by providing her with a home.

He tried to recall all the reasons that was a terrible idea. Her ridiculous teddy-bear collection. Her insistence on fixing proper meals. The undercurrent of sex appeal that might lead them both into an unsuitable liaison.

A very bad idea, all in all. Still, they'd rubbed along well enough at Renée's house.

He'd give it more consideration a little later on.

Right now, he needed to take care of Brooke. Although she was smiling at the camera, she definitely looked pale.

Finally the reporter departed. Jane glanced at her watch. "I'm afraid I'm late for appointments or I'd offer to examine you."

"That's not necessary." Brooke turned her head—and winced.

"At least let me prescribe a painkiller. You must hurt like crazy." Jane dug into her purse.

Brooke massaged the back of her neck. "Thanks, but I can't take medication."

"Why not?" Oliver asked.

"Because I might be pre…" She halted midword.

"You're pregnant?" Jane asked, clearly startled.

"I didn't mean to… Well, sort of."

Oliver stared at Brooke in disbelief. The girl had a gift for landing in hot water *and* for denying reality. "Are you or aren't you?"

"I'm not sure. Can we count that as a big maybe?"

She had no more sense than a cantaloupe. "You charged

right at the guy! Didn't it occur to you that you might rupture something?"

"I'm fine," Brooke insisted.

"How far along are you?" Jane inquired. "I'm an obgyn, in case you didn't know."

"My last period was two or three months ago. I'm kind of irregular."

"Have you had any bleeding or cramping since you tackled that man?" Jane asked her.

Brooke shook her head and cringed. "Ow."

"You should see your doctor as soon as possible. You do have one, don't you?" Jane continued. "If not, my partner and I can treat you."

"My job provides benefits. But it's been a while since I've had a checkup," Brooke admitted. "I guess I should take the pregnancy test I bought."

"Please do." Jane fished in her pocket and produced a business card. "I don't consider it wise to treat friends, but I recommend Sean—my partner, Dr. Sawyer. We'll waive any deductible on your insurance."

"Wow. Thanks." Brooke tucked the card into her pocket.

"I'd recommend taking acetaminophen—Tylenol— right away," Jane told her. "It's safe during pregnancy. You should avoid anything containing aspirin, as that can contribute to bleeding."

"Thanks."

"You won't delay about making an appointment?"

"I promise."

After Jane left, Oliver helped Brooke inside his house, and there she sank onto the rented couch beside him. "Dr. Salonica gave you the afternoon off," he told her. "Do you want to rest here for a while or should I drive you back to Renée's? I can pick up some Tylenol, if you need it."

She rubbed her neck. "I'm sure Renée will have a bottle in the medicine cabinet. Just give me a minute to start moving."

Impulsively he said, "Turn around."

"What?"

"Turn your back to me."

Mystified, she obeyed. Flexing his hands, he yielded to his instinct to touch her and began to work on her shoulders. The sooner he eased the tension from her muscles, the less they were going to hurt later on.

Bit by bit, her stiffness loosened beneath his hands. Soft hair drifted over his fingers. Brooke smelled as if she'd eaten something delicious for lunch, Oliver thought, inhaling cinnamon and a trace of orange. Probably he should have eaten lunch, too, because if he wasn't careful, he might start nibbling on *her*.

As he probed the vulnerable curve of her spine, Oliver's fingers found a whole series of knots and teased them away. He enjoyed bringing her pleasure. How sweet she was.

Very brave. And out of her mind. She was half the size of that creep, and yet she hadn't hesitated to tackle him.

By the time Oliver finished, Brooke was practically melting. He hated to disturb her, but he was already late for an appointment. "May I drive you home?"

She sighed and pulled her thoughts back to reality. "It's just around the block, and my car's here."

"Sure you feel okay to get behind the wheel?"

"I'm from Southern California. I was born driving." Brooke smiled. "Any time you feel like giving me a massage, however, I'll be happy to cooperate."

Oliver grinned back. "Maybe tonight. Also, there's something I want to discuss with you." He hadn't intended to say that. But under the circumstances, her need for protection seemed considerable.

"It isn't a lecture about safe sex, is it?" she asked.

"Do I look like the kind of person who goes around lecturing about safe sex?"

She laughed. "Okay. And I promise."

"Promise what?"

"Not to cook dinner."

When his stomach rumbled, he regretted shooting his mouth off about that. Well, he didn't expect her to cook tonight, in any event. "No problem."

At the very least, he'd find out the result of her pregnancy test. And if good judgment didn't overwhelm his instincts, he might just invite this woman to move in with him.

"IT'S PINK." Brooke paced the den.

From the sofa, Renée regarded her with sympathy. "What're you going to do?"

Brooke wondered if someone could have tampered with the test kit. Maybe she'd thrown it off by moving it from place to place.

Yeah, right. Even her world-class talent for self-deception couldn't buy that excuse.

She had officially committed the stupidest act of her life. She'd let Kevin make her pregnant.

Physical misery added to Brooke's grumpiness. Acetaminophen and a massage hadn't entirely erased the soreness in her upper body, and now her stomach roiled as if it had never heard about the *morning* part of morning sickness.

"Options?" she inquired without much hope.

"There's Kevin. He has legal obligations." Renée didn't sound too hopeful about the prospect of Kevin fulfilling those.

"I don't even want him to find *out* about this!" Brooke grabbed a teddy bear and hugged it as she paced. For some reason, the furry little body soothed her. "He needs to make his marriage work for his daughters' sake, and this would ruin everything."

"*Your* baby deserves a father, too," Renée pointed out.

"Yes, but not Kevin." Okay, she couldn't change biology. "I mean…I wish I'd realized what kind of person he is. He lied about his wife to manipulate me and then he stole the rent money. I don't respect him, Renée, and I certainly don't want him messing up my kid's life."

"Still…" The doorbell rang. "Expecting someone?"

"Maybe Oliver."

The blonde swung to her feet. "Is this a personal conversation? Should I disappear?"

"It's your house. And don't get up."

"Too late. Take it easy, Mom."

Brooke would have preferred some other, more appropriate title. Like Fleabrain or Meathead.

When Oliver followed Renée into the family room, he looked so solid and warm that longing tugged at Brooke. She had an instant sense memory of his hands caressing her body this afternoon, and she yearned for more.

Deep inside, a primitive instinct took in that thick, dark hair and well-toned body and screamed *Daddy!* It must be the hormones. Because it couldn't be her brain.

"How're you feeling?" Oliver asked.

"Sore."

From the fridge, Renée retrieved the salad she'd brought home for dinner. "She's pregnant."

"Thanks for the discretion," Brooke grumbled.

"You already told him you might be," her friend replied.

Oliver paused on the step between kitchen and den. "It's for sure?"

Holding the teddy bear in front of her face, Brooke said in a high voice, "The stick turned pink." As pink as her cheeks, she thought in embarrassment.

"She refuses to tell Kevin," Renée informed their guest. "She doesn't want to screw up his reconciliation. Also, she's finally figured out he's a jerk, which is one step in the right direction."

"What're you—my mouthpiece?" Brooke challenged.

"Better than a stuffed animal." Oliver folded his arms. "This isn't going to stay secret for long. You realize people at work will notice."

A horrible idea struck Brooke. She tossed the bear aside, no longer comforted by the toy. "Helen Salonica might think it's her husband's baby!"

Sitting at the table, Renée regarded Brooke with exasperation. "Don't get bent out of shape. You can always take a DNA test. Besides, once it's born I'm sure it won't look anything like old baldy."

"Yes, but it might look like Kevin. What a cruel fate."

Oliver scowled. "You're both ignoring the obvious."

"Why don't you spell it out for us?" Renée asked.

"The responsible thing to do is give the baby up for adoption."

"I will not!" Until she spoke, Brooke hadn't realized how strongly she felt.

Theoretically, she believed in adoption. After parting bitterly with her stepfather while she was struggling through community college, she'd shared crowded apartments with several single moms. Although they'd loved their kids, the pressures of parenthood and poverty had been exhausting. She'd heard too much yelling and seen too many youngsters left unsupervised. Children deserved parents who were mature enough and stable enough to cope with them.

But the moment Brooke glimpsed that pink stick, tenderness had filled her heart, along with a sharp understanding of what it meant to become a mother. That her life was about to mean far more than merely stumbling from one day to the next.

She'd experienced an unexpected sense of connection to her own mother, and she missed her with painful intensity. At least there was a little of Marlene in this child. Maybe a lot. And of Brooke's dad, whom she'd lost much too young.

By some miracle, they were going to live on into another generation. No way would she give up her baby unless she had to.

Oliver continued, oblivious. "Now that my choice of roommate has proved, shall we say, unfortunate, I'd be happy to let you move in. I can't afford to offer a room rent-free but I can discount—"

"That's okay," Brooke interjected. "I know you're strapped, what with two house payments and all."

Renée raised an eyebrow.

"Well, he *is*." Brooke wouldn't consider living there for free. She'd feel like a leech.

"You'll need to make other arrangements before the baby's born. I don't have the patience to share quarters with a screaming infant. And neither, I suspect, do you," Oliver said.

Brooke bristled. "I'll be a wonderful mother!"

"Have you planned more than a few months into the future?" he demanded. "This is a twenty-year commitment."

"Nobody thinks that far ahead. Or if they do, they miss all the fun in between," she snapped.

"What do you think will happen when this kid reaches adolescence? Do you feel equipped to provide guidance and discipline?" Oliver persisted. "A baby isn't a toy."

Did he have to be so supercilious? He reminded Brooke of a teacher she'd had, who'd nagged that if she didn't improve her grades, she'd never qualify for a college scholarship. The fact that he'd been right just made her angrier.

Oliver was *not* right. He couldn't be.

Brooke glared. "Does moving in with you mean I have to listen to sermons day and night?"

"You can't expect me to sit back and let you ignore reality."

"To heck with your house!" Brooke stormed. "You'd rather see me enter a home for unwed mothers, anyway."

His jaw tightened. "Don't you have relatives who could help?"

"You mean, like my stepfather?" Brooke disliked even speaking about the man. "You'd love him. He's a total miser, with the warmth of an iceberg."

"Sometimes people come through in a crisis," Renée suggested.

Tears pricked her eyes. "Not him. My mom felt lousy for a whole year before he let her see a doctor, and then she died of ovarian cancer. If they'd diagnosed it sooner, she might have lived."

Oliver blew out a long breath. "Brooke, I didn't mean to open old wounds. You're welcome to room with me till the baby's born. It would be irresponsible of me to encourage you to drift after that."

"So you'll turn me into the street?" Maybe she was being unfair, but the man's attitude infuriated her.

"The offer remains open for a week. By then, you'll have to make some sort of decision about where to stay." With a rueful nod, he went out.

Brooke grabbed the bear and hugged it again. Useless. A giant knot seemed to have formed inside her chest.

Then she got an idea. Not a well-formed idea, but the glimmerings of one that might allow her to keep her baby and have a happy ending, after all.

That would show Oliver.

Chapter Seven

Oliver spent Thursday playing catch-up. Yesterday's close call at his house and the demands associated with the re-building of his condo mustn't be allowed to interfere with his business.

At lunchtime he was surprised to receive a call from Winston Grooms. The developer didn't bother with small talk. "I just learned there's going to be a home owners' association meeting Sunday night to discuss legal action against our plans for the cottage. Heard anything about that?"

"I didn't have a chance to read my mail yesterday," Oliver admitted. "I'm sorry to hear about it."

Although his professional involvement with the cottage had ended once escrow had closed, he was still willing to lend support to his former clients. Technically that was client—singular—since Sherry alone had purchased the cottage, but Oliver knew that she planned to add Winston to the title after their marriage.

"It's short notice. I believe our opponents are trying to catch us off guard." The man released an impatient breath. "I'd rather send a lawyer, but Sherry thinks we ought to hear them out in person."

Sunday night. Oliver checked the schedule on his digital organizer. "What time?"

"Eight o'clock."

"I'll be there. By the way, I'd like to talk to you about the resort." Although Oliver didn't have a million bucks to invest, Winston might appreciate his promotional ideas for the project. Oliver wasn't sure what role he could play, but he was determined to find out.

"Great!" The man's tone brightened. "I was sorry you took off so fast after my presentation." They agreed to a meeting the following week at Winston's office in nearby Fullerton.

After hanging up, Oliver wolfed down a sandwich. Usually, when he had a spare moment, his daydreams focused on successful investments and seeing his name in *Forbes* magazine. But now they drifted to last night's quarrel with Brooke.

He hadn't meant to criticize her half-baked idea about raising a child alone. Although it *was* half-baked, he knew he must have sounded ungracious after the favor she'd just done him.

Why had he harped on the notion of kicking her out as soon as she gave birth? That had been downright churlish.

When he'd finished his lunch, he repaired to the florist shop at one end of the Archway Center. From the refrigerated case, he selected a basket of pink and yellow roses with some other tiny blue flowers amid a sprawl of ferns.

"Who's the client?" asked the florist, Juanita, who often put together arrangements for him.

"Oh, it isn't business. It's a thank-you for saving my butt."

She displayed a range of cards. "Oh, it's for Brooke."

"Does *everyone* know about that?" He chose a card bedecked with teddy bears.

"It was in the paper this morning." The florist tied a bright yellow bow around the basket and attached Oliver's note. "She's quite a heroine. That doctor could have been killed."

All because he'd failed to screen his rental applicant properly. Guilt added to Oliver's determination to make amends. "That's true."

"She'll enjoy this."

Oliver paid, thanked Juanita and proceeded down the walkway. He hadn't had time to read the newspaper before work.

Dr. Salonica was taking full advantage of the publicity, Oliver discovered when he reached the orthodontist's office. In the front window a computer-printed banner declared, "Smile Central Employee Saves the Day!"

Beneath it, someone had clipped the article and pasted it onto black poster board. It painted a picture of heroism and bravery, as related by Jane and the police officers. The accompanying photo captured both Jane and Brooke's vulnerability. Oliver's chest tightened as he thought about how events might have turned lethal.

Inside, several women leafed through magazines as they waited for their children. Balloons bobbed above the reception desk, tied to the handle of an enormous flower arrangement that obscured Brooke. Birds of paradise, calla lilies and orchids. Impressive.

Leaning on the counter, Oliver set his own offering in front of her, wishing he'd opted for a larger display. "Who sent that?"

Bright green eyes peered up at him. "Jane. Beautiful,

huh?" Holding his roses close to her nose, she inhaled. "These are fabulous. Thanks."

"You're more than welcome."

The other receptionist stared at him sourly. Long, stringy hair did nothing to flatter her thin face, and neither did her heavy-rimmed glasses. This, Oliver gathered, must be the "friend" who'd canceled plans to share an apartment. He waited until she was busy on the phone to murmur to Brooke, "Any chance she's changed her mind about sharing her place?"

Brooke chuckled. "She's so jealous she could spit. But no."

Well, the envious woman's loss might be his gain. "Any chance I could talk to you alone for a sec?"

She waggled a can of lemon-lime soda. "Sure. This is empty. I was about to head to the break room for a replacement."

"My treat." He couldn't resist adding, "I'm a big spender."

"All donations gratefully accepted."

They crossed a large, cheery room where technicians labored over openmouthed teenagers and a few adults. In their midst, Nicholas Salonica caught sight of the visitors and waved a metal instrument in salute.

The break room resembled lunchrooms everywhere, with vending machines, sturdy tables and the inevitable coffeepot, microwave oven and refrigerator. "I don't suppose they sell milk, do they?" Oliver asked.

"I guess I'd better start thinking for two," Brooke conceded. "Okay, that would be great."

He bought her a container. "Found a place to live yet?"

"I have several possibilities." She inserted a straw.

"They do *not* include hitting up Jane, in case you were about to suggest it."

"Why not?" The doctor had a four-bedroom house.

"Because that would be taking advantage," she shot back. "Don't you ask her, either."

"I have no intention of it, because I'm hoping you'll forgive my rudeness last night," Oliver said.

"Is that an apology?"

Did she have to rub it in? "You could take it that way."

"Or I could take it some other way," Brooke observed wryly. "I wish Sherry LaSalle had gone for my proposal to house-sit her cottage. It's such a ridiculous waste, letting it sit there empty."

Her spirit floored him. Brooke had had the nerve to approach Helen Salonica's best friend? "When did you talk to her?"

"Right before I spotted the rip-off artist at your house. She was checking on her property, so I stopped to discuss security concerns."

"How'd that go?"

She contemplated her milk as if it might contain the secrets of the universe. "We had a little argument. Or rather a yelling and me-stomping-back-to-my-car argument."

"Of course you did." He could have predicted that. Still, sometimes fortune favored the bold. "At least you tried."

"In light of your peace offering," Brooke said, "I've decided to reconsider your offer."

He performed a quick mental shuffle to absorb the fact that she'd saved him the trouble of asking. "You nixed the home for unwed mothers?"

Her nose wrinkled. "Go ahead and make fun of the handicapped. Temporarily handicapped, anyway."

Belatedly Oliver glanced around and was grateful to see no one within earshot. "I apologize for being so high-handed. Whatever decision you go with, at least I can ensure that you're somewhere safe and comfortable while you're pregnant." As a final inducement, he added, "You can cook if you want to. I might even eat with you once in a while."

Brooke beamed. "You're cute when you're humble. Too bad it doesn't happen more often."

"Is that a yes?" he inquired.

"Definitely."

From his pocket, Oliver produced a spare key. "You can move in whenever it suits you."

"Tomorrow night, okay? The remodeling doesn't start till Monday, but Renée's clearing out her furniture for the construction crew this weekend."

"No problem."

"What's the rent? I'll write you a check."

Impulsively, Oliver said, "The first month is free."

"You don't have to do that." At such close range, her large green eyes mesmerized him.

He broke the spell with an offhand response. "What can I say? I have a big heart."

"Thanks. I'm hoping I won't have to stay more than a couple of months. I have this plan."

"What kind of plan?" Oliver doubted she'd devised any sort of practical method of supporting herself and a child.

"I'll tell you on Friday."

He consulted the wall clock. Better get moving. "Does this plan involve Kevin?"

"Nope."

"That's good." The fellow owed her support, and the

child had a right to know its father. In every other respect, however, Brooke was better off without that loser. "You ought to run this by me before you take any further steps."

"Don't worry. I will."

A dental technician entered and eyed them suspiciously while removing a paper sack from the fridge. Oliver gave up the battle. "See you tomorrow night."

Brooke raised her milk carton. "Till then." And gave him a smile mischievous enough to curl his toes.

Sauntering out, Oliver wondered what sort of merry chase he'd let himself in for by agreeing to room with her. As for her plan, well, knowing Brooke, he could only brace himself for the unexpected.

BY FRIDAY EVENING, Renée had packed the contents of her china cabinet into boxes, which she stored in the garage, and she was preparing the rest of her furniture for removal to a storage facility. Brooke fixed a clean-out-the-freezer meal of salmon, asparagus, waffles, pasta salad and orange sherbet.

"Creative menu," her friend observed as she indulged in a serving of waffles topped with sherbet. "Tasty, too."

"Thanks for giving me the canned food." Brooke had scored a hefty supply of corn, spaghetti sauce, olives, soup and mushrooms. "Oliver and I'll be eating that for weeks."

"I can't remember why I bought it. I never cook."

"You're welcome to join us for meals now and then. You and Tess, both."

She hoped that her reluctance to invite Renée's neighbor and soon-to-be hostess didn't show too much. Tess Phipps, a hard-edged divorce attorney, had nothing good to say about men, and after all, Brooke *was* staying with Oliver.

"Thanks, but it's back to a liquid diet for me." Renée

stirred salmon flakes into the pasta salad. She chowed down with a vengeance whenever she went off her regimen. "I wish I could be a fly on the wall, though. I love watching you and Olé squabble."

"Olé?" Brooke repeated. "Is that a pet nickname?"

"Used to be." Renée showed no trace of wistfulness. She'd never been the sentimental type. "You two sure strike sparks off each other. I've never believed that opposites attract, but you guys are living proof."

"Me and Oliver, attracted?" Brooke hooted. "You're kidding."

While she got pleasantly shivery around the guy, he treated her like a kid sister. Besides, he acted annoying far more often than he acted endearing.

"He's good-looking." Renée munched a forkful of asparagus. "You could do worse."

"That's faint praise. Besides, *you* broke up with him, so you can't find him all that wonderful."

"We were too much alike," Renée explained. "And he's a workaholic. Talk about boring."

"Oliver's never boring," Brooke said. "A bit stodgy, but you just have to poke him in the right places to get him moving."

"Like a skunk holed up under the house?" Her friend chuckled. "What an image!"

"Oliver's not a skunk." He had acted grouchy on occasion, Brooke recalled. "A porcupine, maybe."

Renée pushed away from the table. "I'll have to jog an extra hour to work that off. Thanks for cooking."

"My pleasure. You have no idea how much I appreciate your putting up with me these past few weeks," Brooke responded.

"It was one week and a couple of days. The entertainment value has been more than worth it," Renée assured her. "See you around."

Her friend's exit cut off any protracted farewells. Despite her outgoing nature, Renée had limited tolerance for emotional moments.

Her upbringing must have been difficult. Except for the fact that she'd grown up in San Diego and had lived in Huntington Beach for a while, she'd never mentioned anything about her past to Brooke.

You had to respect a person's distances. Even your closest friend's.

Once the dishes were put away, throwing clothes in a suitcase didn't take Brooke long. She and Kevin had rented their furniture, and her kitchen and bathroom appliances fit into one large box, while the bears filled another. After she'd packed a few sacks of food and her computer, she was ready to go. Unable to find Renée on the premises, she locked up and left a note.

She curved around the U, past the cottages. At number ten an elderly woman rocked on the porch, watching children playing nearby. That must be Minnie Ortiz. She sure had a pleasant face.

Approaching Oliver's house, Brooke spotted Jane McKay walking a lop-eared spaniel. They arrived in front of their respective houses at the same moment.

"Moving in?" the doctor asked. "Please let me help. Don't worry about Stopgap. He's a pussycat—in a manner of speaking."

Brooke scratched the pooch behind the ears. "Why'd you name him Stopgap?"

"When I bought him, I figured he'd keep me company

until I had a husband and kids. Although now I'm beginning to think that may never happen. Guess I should have named him Life Companion."

"You're way too young to give up." Brooke retrieved food from her rear seat. "You should launch a campaign to meet new people."

"Oh, I'm too shy for that." Jane removed the sacks of canned goods from her grasp. "I'll take those. And speaking of meeting people, I hope you'll come to a potluck dinner with me. It's Sunday night at six. You don't have to bring anything."

"I enjoy cooking." They let themselves inside, where the air pressure sent creaks echoing through the house. Oliver wasn't around, Brooke noted with a twinge of disappointment.

"Please—you're my guest," Jane protested. "It's a group of women who live on the street. We call ourselves the Foxes, for Females Only–Exuberantly Single, although one member, Diane, got married last winter. Renée attends, too, and you might know some of the others."

If all the unmarried women on Harmony Road participated, that could present a problem. "I'm afraid Sherry LaSalle doesn't like me. She might object to my attending."

Jane snorted. "Everybody dislikes *her,* so you'll be in great company. She's definitely not among the Foxes. In fact, after we eat, we're going to a home owners' association meeting to scream and yell about the cottage. You can join us in glaring at her."

Brooke still felt a bit sorry for the heiress. How miserable to be an outcast. "Since I'm not a permanent resident, I'll watch from the sidelines. But the dinner should be fun."

"Great!" On their second trip to the car, Jane hefted

the computer. "We meet at Alice Watson's, right across the street."

"Gee, such a long walk." Brooke took out her suitcase and closed the trunk.

"She and Tess Phipps are on the association board, by the way. We're a powerful group," Jane explained.

"I'm impressed." Brooke wasn't sure she belonged with such an accomplished bunch of women. Still, she'd be Jane's guest.

"By the way, have you scheduled an appointment with Sean yet?"

Oh, yes, the obstetrician…needles and examinations and pills large enough to choke a horse.

"Your receptionist said she'd fit me in right after I get off work Wednesday. Thanks." The dog, which had waited on the porch, thumped its tail as they edged by. "Too bad this pooch wasn't around when that bad guy grabbed you."

"Stopgap? He'd have run and hidden in the bushes." With a chuckle, Jane shouldered her way inside and set down Brooke's computer.

Brooke hoped her new friend might stick around for a while. Jane pleaded weariness, however, and off she went with Stopgap dragging on his leash.

After stowing perishables in the refrigerator, Brooke studied the layout of her new quarters. The kitchen was at the front of the house and had a lovely bay window. The living room flowed into the den, which in turn opened onto an office.

The airy design of the interior admitted lots of light, an effect that was enhanced by the fresh neutral paint. Brooke would have picked a brighter color than beige, but she knew that was standard for rental properties.

Hoping Oliver wouldn't mind, she wandered into the bedroom wing and checked out the largest chamber. The rented furnishings consisted of a king-size bed and matching dresser. Alluring traces of Oliver's masculine scent wafting from the bedding caught her attention.

She was reminded that this was where he slept. Where he padded around in his underwear while shaving, broad shoulders bare, hair tousled. Where he…brought his dates and tumbled them onto these sheets?

Her chest tightened. No way! He wouldn't do that.

Yet why should she object? She'd never minded his going out with Renée. But that was before they'd spent so much time together. Before she'd come to regard him as a mentor and something more.

Simple human vulnerability was making her see him in a different light, Brooke supposed. A light she'd better switch off right now. If there'd ever been an utterly incompatible male for her, it was Oliver.

Brooke pushed the matter from her mind. Time to get settled and fix a meal before her stomach growled so loud the neighbors complained about the noise.

Opposite the master suite lay the guest room. Her room.

Brooke hauled in her suitcase and began stowing clothes and toiletries. The bed might be narrow and the bureau slightly atilt, but she loved the window facing the street, with a view that encompassed the whole curve of Harmony Road.

Although it was just around the bend and up the hill, Renée's house had felt isolated. Here, Brooke seemed to be in the thick of things.

Humming, she emerged from the room and positioned her bears around the den. The place seemed warmer. But still not warm enough.

Where was Oliver? Real-estate agents worked long hours. Without realizing she was doing it, she'd envisioned being housemates as one unending pajama party. She'd also looked forward to discussing the plan that had been taking shape in her mind all day.

Disappointed, Brooke plopped down in front of the TV. Tonight, the reality-show contestants all seemed foolish and the dramas were boring, and Brooke dozed off.

She awoke to the grating sound of the front door being pulled open. It was—quick check of her watch—quarter to ten.

In blew the lord of the manor, shirt rumpled, tan blazer bearing a greasy splotch, testimony to dinner on the run, and a cell phone clamped to his ear with one hand. In the other hand, Oliver lugged a laptop case.

"Do you have to use that lender?" he was demanding. "The last escrow we did with them closed two weeks late because they lost the paperwork. Sure, it's your client's choice. Fine. Now another thing…" Giving Brooke the briefest of nods, he headed for his office.

How much later could he work? The man had to take a break sometime.

Determined to wait a while longer, she fetched a glass of milk from the kitchen and propped her feet on the coffee table. Then she turned up the volume on the TV so he wouldn't forget she was around.

At long last Oliver emerged from the office, stuffing a doughnut into his mouth. Where had *that* come from?

"Isn't that stale?" Brooke inquired. "I could make you an omelet." She'd developed a bit of an appetite herself, she discovered.

"Don't bother. Moved in okay?"

"Yes. My room's perfect." She cleared space for him on the sofa. "Do you have a minute?"

As he sat down he frowned at the bears festooning every spare surface. What did he think they were going to do—poop on the furniture? "How many of those did you say Kevin gave you?"

"Three. Why do you care?"

"All at once or for separate occasions?"

"Uh…separate." Despite his grandiose promises to drape her in jewels and fly her to the South Seas, Kevin's occasional gifts had been limited to stuffed animals. At least he hadn't charged *those* to Dr. Salonica. As far as she knew.

Not much to show for a relationship of eight months. But at least, unlike their donor, these bears would never desert her.

"Put them out of sight, would you?" Oliver growled. "Seeing all that clutter drives me crazy."

An evening-long wait and all he could do was snipe? "*You* drive *me* crazy," Brooke retorted, and gathering an armful of bears, she stalked to her room.

As soon as she was alone, to her utter humiliation, she burst into tears.

Chapter Eight

Good lord. All he'd done was ask her to put a few bears back in her room. So the rumors were true about pregnant women being emotional wrecks.

Leaning back on the sofa, Oliver closed his eyes. He'd had a rough day, his feet hurt and that doughnut was sitting in his stomach like a rock.

In her bedroom, Brooke was probably crying her eyes out. Or throwing darts at the wall and cursing his name.

Oliver wished he didn't have to deal with this. He preferred his life neat and compartmentalized, which was why he'd sought a male housemate. Maybe if he pretended she didn't exist…

Sure. Right. He should have kept his mouth shut about the bears. She'd had enough insensitive cads in her life.

He dragged himself upright and went to check on her.

The first thing Oliver noticed on entering her room was the bright pink comforter printed with black-and-white cats. If the woman ever suffered a hangover, she'd have burned that long ago.

Second, he registered that she was sitting cross-legged on the bed with a pad on her lap. "Writing in your diary?" he asked.

When she looked up, the sight of her tear-streaked face tugged at his conscience. Damn! Oliver hated guilt.

"Making a list," she said.

"Of ways to torment me?" he joked. No smile. "Okay, forget that. Put the bears anywhere you like."

"You hurt their feelings," she told him.

"I hurt *their* feelings?"

"Whenever I look at them, I'll remember you yelling at me."

Guilt twisted through him. "I didn't yell. Did I?"

"Well, you snarled."

"I'm sorry. It's Friday, it's late and I just wasn't prepared for stuffed animals everywhere I looked. How about giving me a break?" He waved a hand as if erasing those words on an invisible blackboard. With Brooke, honesty seemed to work. "The truth is, they remind me of that jerk, Kevin, and he ticks me off."

She blinked away the tears. "So you only object to the ones Kevin gave me?"

He considered. "I suppose that's mostly true."

"I can handle that. I'll keep them in here." She patted the bed. "Sit down—I need your help with something."

Normally, when a woman invited Oliver to sit on her bed, he had a pretty good idea of her intentions. Brooke mystified him.

He perched on the edge, wishing the furniture-rental place had sent him a double, instead of a twin for the spare room. Still, it seemed the right size for her sheets. "Is this bed too small?"

"It's fine." She favored him with a watery smile. "Beats a sleeping bag in my car."

"You've done that?" he asked, shocked. While he assumed she'd had it tough in the past, he hadn't imagined she'd ever been homeless.

"Once or twice." She refocused on the pad. "Now, about this. As you know, strategizing isn't my strong point."

"Indeed."

"Still, in a few months I'm going to be responsible for another human being. So I thought I should come up with a plan."

The only thing scarier than Brooke without a plan might be Brooke *with* one, Oliver mused. While other people might think outside the box, she thought outside the universe.

"This ought to be interesting." Leaning closer, he tilted his head to read the list. She'd numbered the lines from one to ten but hadn't filled anything in. "What do you have in mind?"

"I've decided to get married."

Exhaustion must have blurred his hearing, or maybe he'd missed a major detail. "Married to whom?"

"That's the issue," she replied, as if this was a logical conversation. "I have to quit messing around with Mr. Wrongs and find Mr. Right. That's where you come in."

"Me?" He issued an audible gulp.

"Not as the groom." She whacked his arm with the pad. "But if I'm ever going to make it down the aisle, I need your help."

In that moment of utter loopiness, Oliver thought he understood why Brooke hugged teddy bears. He felt like squeezing something right now. Her, for looking so sweet. Or… Wait. Being around her was exerting a pernicious effect on his common sense. He should be reading her the riot act over this nonsense, not playing along.

"You can't mean Kevin," Oliver began.

"Of course not. He's already got a wife. Besides, talk about poor husband material!"

"Agreed."

"He belongs in the Mr. Wrongs column, except I don't have a column for that. Hmm. I can't even figure out how to organize this—which demonstrates why I won't be able to do it without you."

Oliver hated to belabor the obvious, but someone had to. "Brooke, you can't just decide to get married. For one thing, you aren't dating anyone, unless you've been keeping me in the dark on the subject. Second, you're pregnant. That's quite an obstacle to starting a new relationship."

"The right guy wouldn't mind that," she said. "He'd love me in spite of it. Maybe *because* of it. Suppose he's been longing for a child and he had mumps or something and can't be a father. This would be perfect."

"Reality check."

She tapped her pen against the pad. "Okay. I get carried away sometimes with my scenarios. That *could* happen, though, right?"

He should have stayed in the den while he'd had the chance, Oliver thought. "Let's focus here. If I understand this, your goal is to identify, stalk and hog-tie a suitable husband. Is that correct?"

"Sort of. But he's supposed to fall in love with me and think that marrying me is *his* idea." She regarded Oliver expectantly.

"I'm not about to start recruiting potential victims—I mean, husbands—for you."

She glared. "Did I ask you to do that?"

He finger-combed his hair back into place, even though

he didn't plan on going out again tonight. "The list is blank. It's a natural assumption."

"All I'm asking is for you to vet the guys I find," Brooke said. "You couldn't see past your housemate's credit report to recognize the feral gleam in his eyes. Well, I can't look past a man paying me compliments and having a thick head of hair without messing around like *this*." Reaching over, she undid his efforts, tickling his scalp until he batted her hand away.

"Hey!" he shouted.

"I enjoyed that." Brooke settled against the head-board. "Well?"

"You seriously believe the solution to your problems is latching on to some man you haven't even met yet?"

"You're a successful real-estate agent. Don't you believe a person can accomplish anything with a well-thought-out plan, careful execution and diligent work?"

"I can't get past the well-thought-out-plan part," he retorted.

"Just go with it." Her tone took on a ragged edge.

Pregnancy hormones again, Oliver suspected. If he didn't play along, she might burst into tears once more, and he couldn't handle another round of that.

Besides, she appeared to be serious. If he didn't screen the guys, she'd pick another hopeless case. With luck, she'd soon tire of this game and realize he'd been right in the first place. The baby deserved a loving adoptive family.

"Sure," he said. "I'll look them over and render a verdict."

She released a long breath. "That's great!" Biting her lip, she regarded the paper. "Any suggestions to start with?"

"A good night's sleep," Oliver told her. "I'll see you in the morning."

"You aren't working tomorrow?"

"Of course I'm working. But I can spare an hour on a Saturday morning."

"That's your time off?"

"Weekends are busy in real estate. Don't tell me you were counting on my company." While he hated to disappoint this winsome little soul, he wasn't about to change his lifestyle or reduce his income to provide Brooke Bernard with companionship.

"No. I'm already making friends," she chirped. "Jane invited me to have dinner with the Foxes on Sunday."

That *was* an honor. "Congratulations."

Being around mature women ought to do her a world of good. Although Oliver couldn't picture a serious, woman-of-the-world version of Brooke, the Foxes might talk *some* sense into her scattered brain.

He bid her good-night and got a distracted reply. As he left, he heard the scratch of her pen on paper, no doubt listing a name.

He hoped to high heaven it wasn't his.

BROOKE HAD EVERY INTENTION of spending the weekend being productive. Organizing kitchen cabinets, helping Renée prepare for her construction crew and attending garage sales to ferret out a few decorations for Oliver's rather austere house.

However, the combination of an uneasy stomach and a powerful impulse to sleep kept her in bed until ten on Saturday. After eating breakfast, alone, she beat a path to the library and checked out books on pregnancy and baby care, but she didn't get far in her reading before dozing off.

During the afternoon, she jotted down the names of a few men who might qualify for her daddy list and then crossed them out as she thought of impediments, such as girlfriends and bad habits. After another nap, she surveyed the backyard and concluded that she could achieve her dream of planting a vegetable garden.

With April just around the corner, she had the whole summer ahead. A sunny corner should provide plenty of space for…hmm… She reviewed her favorite recipes and decided on tomatoes, squash, basil, peppers, cucumbers, eggplant, beans and lettuce.

Just thinking about digging up the weeds, however, wore her out. A few more minutes contemplating a host of gardening tasks sent her back to bed for another snooze.

Chalk up one accomplishment, anyway—Brooke stored Kevin's gifts out of sight. The purple bear, the panda and the green rabbit gazed up at her sadly from the floor of her closet as she shut them inside.

On Sunday she spent far too long browsing through the newspaper, distracted by her daydreams. Look at the handsome guy in *this* photo or that one. The world was full of potential Mr. Rights.

And likely Mr. Wrongs.

Oliver put in few brief appearances during Brooke's waking hours, and turned up even more often in her dreams. On Saturday morning she registered the fact that he slept in black pajama bottoms, which would have been sexy except that she remembered Renée picking out those pajamas as a gift for him last Christmas.

When he wasn't out buying or selling or doing whatever it was that he did, he walked around talking into a minuscule headset that was linked to his cell phone. To her annoyance she kept responding, in the mistaken belief that he was addressing *her.*

Several times, as Brooke sat scribbling on her pad, Oliver peeked over her shoulder. By Sunday she realized he feared *his* name might appear on the list, and she assured him that she would never in a zillion years include a guy who couldn't tell the difference between working and being home.

"I'll relax when I'm fifty," he informed her. "Rich and fifty."

"You'll be rich, old and alone," she snipped.

"And you'll still be looking for Mr. Right," he shot back. "Oliver Armstrong."

"You're nominating yourself?"

"I've been trying to reach you since yesterday."

"What?" Trying to make sense of his remark, she finally realized he'd just answered an incoming call. *That* was why he'd spoken his name.

She'd fallen for it again. Furious, she pelted him with a stuffed animal.

He retreated into his office. How frustrating. She couldn't even get a good fight out of the guy.

Around six that evening Jane McKay showed up carrying a large casserole. Brooke joined her at the door with a basket of carrot-zucchini muffins. "I *had* to bake something," she explained.

Jane lifted the cloth over the basket. "Mmm. They smell divine."

"What's in your casserole?" Brooke couldn't see through the plastic snap-on lid.

"Chicken, broccoli, spaghetti and peanut butter."

"What an amazing combination. May I have the recipe?" She'd never heard of cooking pasta with peanut butter.

"Don't you want to taste it first?" Jane inquired as they strolled across the street.

"With those ingredients, it *has* to be good. Or at least interesting." According to Brooke's philosophy, anything unusual enough was always worth the effort.

"I'll e-mail the recipe to you tomorrow."

They rang the bell at the trim, one-story house across the street. While waiting on the porch, Brooke cast an appreciative glance at a climbing rosebush that was ablaze with pink-and-orange blossoms. The owner had lavished considerable care on the place, installing multicolored brick pavers, instead of concrete on the walkway, stained-glass panels in the door and solar panels on the roof.

The door opened. "Hello, Jane and guest," said a commanding, pantsuited woman with elegant snowy hair. "I'm Alice Watson."

"This is Brooke Bernard. She saved my life the other day," Jane responded as their hostess ushered them into the marble-floored entryway.

"Yes. I read about it in the paper," their hostess replied rather primly.

"Your home is gorgeous!" Uncertain about what she should do with the muffins, Brooke thrust the basket into Alice's hands.

"Thank you."

The coolness in the older woman's manner puzzled Brooke. "I live across the street," she added. "I'm renting a room from Oliver Armstrong."

"So I've heard."

They moved toward the sound of female voices. Jane strode ahead, while Brooke accompanied Alice.

She struggled to interpret the older woman's silence. Her clothing shouldn't give offense—she'd worn a long skirt and a modest peasant blouse. Perhaps her hostess was aloof by nature, or by training.

"Were you ever in the army?" Brooke asked her.

An eyebrow lifted in surprise. "No. I was principal at the Brea Academy for many years." The private school had a reputation for academic excellence. "Why do you ask?"

"You just seem to have so much…authority," Brooke explained.

"Is that so?"

There was no mistaking the chill in the older woman's manner. "Did I do something to offend you?" Brooke asked. "Wait! You must be a friend of Sherry LaSalle's, right? She hates me."

Alice halted, a tentative smile quivering on her stern face. "You are engaging, I'll admit that. For the record, I have no particular bond with Mrs. LaSalle."

"Is it because I've been parking in front of your house?" Brooke persisted. "Some people are territorial that way. I'll try to watch it."

"I appreciate your eagerness to please," Alice conceded. "However, I have no real attachment to my front curb."

"Then what'd I do?" Brooke crossed her fingers, hoping that her hostess wouldn't deny acting standoffish. If that happened, they'd never bridge the gap.

Following the briefest of pauses, Alice relented. "Jane let slip that you're with child by a married man. Also, you're living with Oliver Armstrong. Call me old-fashioned, but—"

"Oh!" Thank goodness she had a chance to clear that up. "My ex-boyfriend was separated from his wife—and he lied about the details of that, by the way. As for Oliver, we aren't even close to being romantically involved. He's just a friend, and a grouchy one at that."

"I see." The older woman appeared to thaw. "But also, do you know Renée Trent?"

"Sure. She's a good friend."

"Are you aware that she used to date Oliver?"

"You're worried that my staying with Oliver might hurt her?" Brooke had misjudged this woman. Alice wasn't cold; she was merely trying to protect other people's feelings. "I was staying with her until two days ago. She urged me to move in with him. You're so kind to worry about her."

Approval glinted in Alice's eyes. "You have a good heart. Perhaps you've made a few errors in judgment, but I always forgave my students their mistakes as long as I believed in them."

"I'm not sure I deserve to have you believe in me," Brooke conceded. "I was never good at coloring inside the lines. But even though I mess up a lot, I try to live by the Golden Rule."

"Welcome to my house." Alice sounded as if she meant it now.

IN THE KITCHEN, wonderful smells greeted Brooke—along with half a dozen women. Brooke recognized the oldest as Minnie Ortiz. Another woman, whose age she placed at around seventy, Lois Oldham, turned out to be the mother of two younger women, Diane Lorenz, who'd recently married contractor Josh Lorenz, and Sarah Oldham, her younger sister.

Everyone, it seemed, had heard of Brooke's heroism, which had been embellished by the neighborhood rumor mill. Brooke corrected the impression that she'd performed karate moves on the evildoer and held him pinned against the car till the police arrived.

When Tess Phipps and Renée joined the group, the conversation shifted to a discussion of Renée's remodeling plans. Last to arrive was a fiftyish woman named Cynthia Lieberman, whom Jane introduced as a psychologist.

An obstetrician. An attorney. A retired school principal. What a remarkable group.

Feeling a little intimidated, Brooke resolved to listen and keep her mouth shut. She soon discovered, however, that despite their imposing credentials, these women were all pretty down-to-earth. She wished she really belonged to a group like this, with roots that in many cases went back for years.

To her surprise, Diane Lorenz took her aside. "May I get your opinion about something?"

"Sure." Brooke had met Josh's wife through Renée, since their houses faced each other. She'd heard the romantic story of how Diane, a widowed teacher, had fallen in love with a man she'd initially mistrusted, and how their twelve-year-old daughters had become as close as sisters.

"Nick Salonica Junior is in my fourth-grade class at Brea Academy. I understand you work for his father."

"That's right." Brooke had met the chubby boy in passing. She doubted she could offer much insight.

"He's been acting up a lot this year, and…well, I don't mean to pry, but is there anything I should be aware of that might be affecting his behavior?" Diane hurried to add, "I mean, anything that's more or less public knowledge. I'm not asking for confidential information."

"You mean, like family problems?" When the other woman nodded, Brooke said, "It's pretty well-known that his parents fight a lot. If I were their kid, I'd be upset, too."

"That could account for his misbehavior. I was afraid some students might be bullying him, but no one at school has observed anything like that," Diane said. "Thanks."

"You're welcome." Thank goodness the teacher didn't realize that Brooke was at the center of the Salonica's dispute. Okay, that was due to Kevin's duplicity and Dr. Salonica's dishonesty, not her own actions. Still, as much as Brooke resented Helen's accusations, she had to sympathize with their children. And a little bit with a woman so insecure about her marriage.

They rejoined the group. Busy filling plates at the counter and carrying them into the dining room, the others didn't seem to have noticed the separate conversation.

At the long, cloth-covered table, Brooke chose a corner seat next to Sarah Oldham. Diane's sister appeared the closest to her in age, and with her mom, she occupied the house next door to Oliver's on the opposite side from Jane. Being neighbors gave them a little extra in common, and for a while they chatted about gardening.

Side conversations dwindled, and the discussion veered to their hostess's romantic dilemma. Alice—as Sarah explained quietly to Brooke—had reconnected with a man who'd broken their engagement half a century earlier.

He'd joined the army and then married a woman overseas. Now widowed, he'd reconnected with his former love, who'd remained single, through the Internet. For the past few months, they'd been sorting through old misunderstandings and discovering the things they had in common.

"I enjoy square dancing, which I'd never have learned if it weren't for George," Alice told the group. "And we have far more in common than I'd have expected after all these years. The problem is that he wants more."

"Men always want more," Tess observed darkly.

"I don't mean sex. Although I'm sure he... Well, let's not go there."

People that age still had sex? That was another bit of information to add to Brooke's understanding of life.

"You mean, he expects greater emotional involvement," Lois filled in.

"You nailed it."

To Brooke, Sarah murmured, "My mom and Alice have been friends for decades. They read each other's minds."

"Is he asking for a commitment?" Renée inquired.

"He mentioned living together," Alice conceded. "I'm not sure I'm willing to surrender my independence. I've lived alone my whole adult life, and I like it."

"That wasn't entirely by choice, though," Lois pointed out. "You'd have married him when you were young."

"Well, I'm not young anymore. I'm fixed in my ways."

"It's human nature to find change threatening," observed Cynthia. The psychologist, Brooke recalled.

"Speaking of change," Alice replied, "we should prepare ourselves for the home owners' meeting."

Although everyone must have noticed the deliberate change of subject, they followed her lead. "You're on the board," Lois said. "I've heard people suggest we hire an attorney and file suit to save the cottage. What do you think?"

"I think it would be expensive," their hostess answered.

"Also, although I don't deal with this sort of thing professionally, in my opinion it'd be difficult to win as long as they're in compliance with city zoning," noted Tess, the lawyer.

Cynthia set down her fork. "Our best bet is psychological warfare. Sherry and Winston need to understand that riding roughshod over the rest of us is going to earn them a lot of enemies. Why would they choose to live in a place where everyone dislikes them?"

"We should present a united front," Diane suggested.

Amid the general agreement, Brooke's spirits sank. These women had been so kind. She wanted to feel that she belonged with them and she did value that adorable little bungalow, yet she kept thinking about Sherry's vulnerability. Despite her high-handed attitude, the woman wasn't a monster.

"I think we should give her a chance," Brooke said.

Heads swiveled in her direction. It was the first time she'd spoken to the whole group, she realized.

"You mean, Sherry?" Tess asked in disbelief.

"You've got to be kidding."

"You obviously don't know the woman."

"She's made it clear she thinks she's better than us."

As reactions flew, Brooke wondered if she'd blown this opportunity. By standing up for Sherry LaSalle, she might have just lost a wonderful group of friends.

She felt like sliding under the table.

Chapter Nine

"You don't think the cottage is worth preserving?" Diane asked.

"Of course I do. I mean, it's beautiful." Brooke wished she dared look to Renée or Jane for support, but it wouldn't be fair to involve them.

"I saw you arguing with Sherry," Minnie told Brooke. "I was sitting on the porch and I heard her say something like, 'I hope Helen makes your life miserable.' I don't know who Helen is, but that's a mean thing to say."

"Helen is Sherry's best friend," Tess filled in. "I ran into her at a service-club meeting. Couldn't stand the woman."

"I'm not saying I'm fond of Sherry." Brooke made no reference to Helen. She'd rather not explain *that* messy situation. "But it's her proposal we're fighting, not her. Do you really want an ongoing feud with a future neighbor? What're you going to do, cold-shoulder her kids when she has them?"

She braced herself for a flood of arguments. Instead, heads nodded reluctantly.

"You're wise beyond your years," Alice told her from the head of the table. "Considering how the woman's treated you, that takes a generous spirit."

Brooke's heart swelled with happiness. Daring to look at Renée and Jane, she saw their smiles of agreement.

"You raise a good point, Brooke," Diane added. "Still, I'm in favor of presenting a united front with the board tonight."

"Against the proposal and not against any individual, correct?" her mother clarified.

"Of course."

"Speaking of proposals…" Brooke hesitated. She ought to keep her mouth shut for a change. On the other hand, Alice already knew about the pregnancy, and it would soon become obvious to everyone. "I have a little plan that I could use some help with. This has nothing to do with the cottage. It's personal."

"A plan?" Renée regarded her.

"It's because, well, I'm pregnant. I think the baby and I would be much better off if I found the right husband, and that isn't likely to happen without some effort on my part."

"You think you can go out and…and *find* a man to marry you, on a timetable?" Jane asked with obvious astonishment.

"Why not? It's worth a try."

Chuckling, Alice shook her head. "You are full of surprises. I have to admire your initiative."

The others appeared uncertain about how they should react. After taking a deep breath, Brooke plunged into her story, which she edited to avoid unnecessary detail and embarrassment. She briefly sketched in the affair with Kevin and explained her determination not to interfere in his attempt to save his marriage.

"This might sound ridiculous," she concluded, "but I believe people can accomplish miracles if they try."

Tears glimmered in Minnie's eyes. "Some of us forget how to believe in miracles, Brooke. I guess we need you to remind us."

"A baby *is* a miracle," Jane agreed.

"What does Oliver think about this?" Renée inquired.

"Despite some initial skepticism—all right, sneering and chortling—he's agreed to test-drive the guys for me. I mean, evaluate them. Because I have such awful judgment."

Everyone laughed. "You're a breath of fresh air, dear," Lois Oldham said.

"I wish I could nominate one of my sons for your list, but they're both married," Minnie put in.

"I wonder if you might have a better chance of stumbling across Mr. Right if you *weren't* looking," Diane said. "That's what happened with Josh and me."

"I'd like to help," her sister chimed in, "but my experiences with men have been almost as bad as yours. I can't think of a single viable specimen."

Tess nodded. "After the divorces I've handled, I'm convinced there's no such thing as Mr. Right."

"Oh, come on, ladies," Cynthia Lieberman scolded them. "Such negativity! Can't we do better than that? She's only requesting names for a list."

"There's a subcontractor that Josh works with," Diane volunteered. "He's kind of cute, and I believe he's single."

On a pad Alice provided, Brooke jotted down his name. Tess suggested a lawyer in her firm. Cynthia mentioned a civil engineer who had an office in the same building as hers.

"Don't forget Bart," Renée prompted.

Brooke searched her memory. "Oh, yeah, the guy next door to you, the gardener. Isn't he kind of old?"

"Not *that* old," replied her friend.

"He looks weathered because he's out in the sun so much," Tess corrected. "He's a year older than me, and I'm thirty-five. We went to high school together here in Brea."

That made him younger than Kevin. Besides, the more Brooke considered, the more she supposed a certain level of maturity might be a plus. "Thanks."

"Have you seen how beautiful his property looks?" Cynthia lived opposite him, Brooke recalled. "He also maintains the lot next door, at number thirteen. The owners leave it vacant for some reason. Thanks to Bart, it's a showplace, on the outside, anyway."

"I *have* noticed. I'd love to learn more about gardening." Brooke had to be practical, though. You couldn't raise a family on beautiful flowers. "How does he earn a living?"

"He's a landscape consultant. With a degree in horticulture." Catching her friends' curious gazes, Tess said, "I've known him for years. Believe me, there are no sparks there."

"Don't protest too much," warned Lois.

"I'm not!"

"I'm sure he'll attend tonight's board meeting," Alice noted. "He comes to almost all our sessions."

"Great. Maybe he can advise me on planting a vegetable garden." Brooke might as well chat with him.

Alice checked her watch. "Speaking of meetings, we should tackle that luscious dessert Diane brought before it's too late."

"My daughter baked a raspberry-chocolate cake for us." Diane collected her mother's and sister's plates. "In case Brooke hasn't heard, Brittany caters baked goods after school."

"Sounds fabulous."

As chairs pushed back, Brooke, too, began gathering dishes. What a great group of women! Instead of rejecting her, they'd done their best to further her plan.

Three names. She was sure there'd soon be more.

IN OLIVER'S EXPERIENCE, home owners' association sessions generally ran half an hour, forty-five minutes, max. Tonight, by contrast, he wouldn't be surprised if they were stuck here until midnight.

He arrived with Winston and Sherry, choosing front-row seats among the several dozen chairs set up in the community clubhouse. For most meetings, that would have been far too many seats. Tonight it left standing room only.

One omission troubled Oliver. Although Josh Lorenz shared his perspective about home owners' rights, the contractor had diplomatically chosen to stay away. His wife, who'd grown up in this development, harbored strong feelings about saving the historic bungalow, and Josh preferred not to cross her.

Diane marched in at the head of the Foxes, with Brooke tagging along beside her. Sherry reacted with a start. "What's *she* doing here? She doesn't even live in the development."

Oliver didn't comment. He'd just as soon Sherry remained ignorant of his relationship to Brooke.

Winston answered his fiancée's question. "Don't you read the paper? She tackled a would-be kidnapper. She's the local heroine." For all his international connections and high-stakes financial dealings, he certainly kept close tabs on events in Orange County. Smart man.

"Nonsense," Sherry muttered. "I'll bet she did nothing more than scream really loud."

Oliver didn't want to think badly of Winston's fiancée. Nevertheless, he enjoyed seeing Brooke's small social triumph prick her pride. She assumed everyone should defer to *her* and she resented being robbed of the spotlight.

Two of the Foxes, Alice Watson and Tess Phipps, joined the remaining three board members at the front table. As the most successful real-estate agent in Harmony Circle, Oliver was well acquainted with them all. In addition to Alice and Tess, they included the board president, retired aerospace engineer Carson Ingalls; Joan Whistler, a home-maker and community volunteer; and J. J. Hughes, an African-American studies professor whose wife, Maryam, ran a day-care center in their home.

In place of a gavel, Carson tapped his pen sharply against the table. "I'm going to outline the situation involving number nine Harmony Road, in case anyone just arrived from the outer parts of the solar system and hasn't heard about it. Then we'll hear comments from the floor. Brief, polite comments, please."

For the next hour debate raged. Should the board hire an attorney to look into filing a lawsuit? Could the association's list of covenants, codes and restrictions—contained in a document signed by all new homebuyers—be amended to prohibit tearing down a livable historic structure?

Following a procession of speakers who urged respect for history and tradition, Oliver presented what he considered a well-reasoned position in support of home owners' rights. Next, Winston pointed out the high cost of fighting this battle in the courts, and assured everyone that while he'd prefer to work this out amicably, he intended to invest as much time and money as necessary to pursue his soon-to-be wife's dream of an ideal home for their future children.

Rafe Montoya provided an acid rebuttal. A monster house would pervert the cozy nature of the block where, across the street, he was raising his orphaned niece and nephew. Did Mrs. LaSalle and Mr. Grooms think their kids, as yet unborn, were more important than his?

Rafe, who'd won an amateur boxing title in high school, looked ready to punch someone. Oliver suspected his cousin's fury in regard to these high-handed newcomers had less to do with the cottage than with the recent deaths of his brother and sister-in-law. Manuel and his wife had died trying to save a stable of horses from a fire, while the wealthy owners of the property had escaped by helicopter. People with money and a sense of entitlement could really drive him wild.

When Rafe took a seat, scattered applause broke out, but then to Oliver's dismay, Sherry stood up. He glanced at Winston, who shrugged. The man almost seemed amused by his fiancée's insistence on speaking. Didn't he realize she might stir up additional antagonism?

"It's ridiculous to blame Winston and me for trying to improve our property," she declared. "Eventually other new buyers will move into a lot of the existing homes, and believe me, they won't be satisfied with tiny houses and outdated architecture. Change is inevitable. Only small-minded people would insist everyone else cling to the past just because that's what suits *them*."

She dropped back into her seat with a satisfied air. At a guess, she was convinced she'd presented an irrefutable case.

An angry buzz rose from the crowd. Oliver caught snippets.

"So we're small-minded, are we?"

"Can't wait for us to be replaced by more snobs like *her,* I see."

"To her, the Taj Mahal is tiny and outdated!"

Sherry looked stunned. "Why are they reacting like this?"

Winston patted her hand. "They'll get over it."

Although tempted to explain that a show of respect toward her new neighbors would be a wise move, Oliver clamped his jaw shut. He felt certain she'd consider such a remark criticism.

Which, of course, it was.

Carson Ingalls raised a hand to restore calm. "The board is going to take a short break. I think we could all use a chance to stretch our legs and reflect on what we've heard."

"I can't stretch my legs. This clubhouse is too tiny," someone quipped. A smattering of laughter broke the tension.

Sherry flushed bright red.

As Oliver got to his feet, he spotted Rafe heading in their direction with steam pouring from his ears. To prevent a public squabble, he left his companions and approached his cousin.

Rafe grumbled, but he allowed Oliver to steer him outside onto the deck. It overlooked the community swimming pool, which sparkled with reflected light from the clubhouse.

The peacefulness of their surroundings didn't seem to affect Rafe's mood. "How can you side with those phonies?" he demanded.

Oliver decided not to challenge the insult. He wasn't here to defend Winston and Sherry personally. "I happen to believe that when you buy a house, you have a right to improve or replace it."

"So you wouldn't mind if they put a fast-food restaurant on the site?" his cousin challenged.

"That's different." Sure, Oliver wouldn't mind being able to trot down the block for a quick burger, but he got Rafe's point. "Since the city's zoned the area as residential, they knew in advance that wasn't allowed. But replacing the house is a legal option."

"It's oversize for the area. It'll wipe out my view and look just plain out of place next to Minnie's cottage." His cousin glared. "I suppose you'd like to see that torn down, as well!"

"I don't want to see anything torn down," Oliver responded.

Fists clenched, his cousin stared toward the clubhouse. "I hate people like them."

"They didn't make any friends tonight," Oliver agreed.

"Yeah." A ghost of a smile appeared at the memory. "Small-minded people? Outdated architecture? That airhead doesn't have a clue how offensive she is."

"Think the Foxes will invite her to join once she moves in?"

His cousin laughed aloud. "Maybe if she puts on an apron and serves dinner to them on bended knees."

Grateful for the change in mood, Oliver asked Rafe about Juan and Sofia. Initially docile and sweet-tempered, the four-year-old twins had grown rambunctious in recent months.

"They're a real handful. The counselor warned me they might act out when our honeymoon period wore off, and she was absolutely right." During their first months together, Rafe had taken the children to an expert. Very wise, in Oliver's opinion.

"Who's babysitting?" he asked.

"My neighbor's daughter. Suzy's good with them, but she's just twelve. She can't take more than an hour or two at a time." Rafe consulted his watch. "I'd love to stay and battle it out, but I've got to get home."

"If you ever get in a bind, I'll be happy to watch them." He could survive a few hours with two preschoolers, Oliver thought.

"Thanks. I might take you up on that." Rafe gave him a light punch on the shoulder. Despite the friendly intentions, it throbbed. "Later, cuz."

"See you." *And remind me, in case I forget, never to get into a knockdown-drag-out with you.*

As he strolled inside Oliver glanced toward Winston, worried that the financier might think he was consorting with the enemy. However, the man appeared too busy conferring with his fiancée to notice anything else.

Renée sauntered over. As usual, she was the most dazzling woman in sight, with her flowing blond hair and statuesque figure. Yet Oliver felt no more than objective admiration. "Rafe's taking this hard, isn't he? Displaced anger, I'd guess."

"Yeah. What the man needs is a wife." Oliver hadn't meant to say that. Still, the kids must be suffering without a mother.

"Oh?" Her eyes widened with interest. "You think he's looking for one?"

This was an unexpected twist. "Don't tell me you've decided independence isn't so hot."

"What?" She blinked, then burst into laughter. "Not for me. For Brooke!"

"Brooke?" Puzzled, he glanced toward his new housemate. A shell-pink sweater emphasized her rounded curves as she twinkled up at Bart Ryan. Why was she being so chummy with that guy?

"I'm sure she told you about her plan to find Mr. Right."

"Well, yes." He'd given that scheme all the consideration it deserved—none. "What's that got to do with anything?"

"Three guesses about why she's flirting with Bart," Renée teased.

Oliver took a closer look at the shaggy, easygoing fellow. A font of information about lawns and landscaping, but…husband material? The prospect disturbed him. Because, well, because the guy wasn't Brooke's type. She'd just be using him to fill one or two of the gaps in her life. "She mentioned wanting to plant a vegetable garden. That might be what they're discussing."

"In any event, it doesn't look as if they're striking any sparks." Renée's remark eased Oliver's grumpiness, although he wasn't sure why. "That's why I suggested Rafe."

"You did what?" She must have lost her mind. "You sicced Brooke onto that misanthrope?"

"I'm not sure what that means."

"Someone who hates other people." That description might be a bit strong for his cousin. Still, the guy'd always had a chip on his shoulder.

"I'm sure he doesn't. Besides, she's so upbeat and nurturing, she'd be great with the kids," Renée observed. "She might sand off a few of his rough edges, too."

Oliver was glad his cousin had left. He didn't care to see Renée matchmaking between two such unsuitable people. "He's wrong for her."

"In what way?"

Oliver's patience snapped. "You're needling me on purpose."

"Just trying to help," she said. "You only invited her to stay with you because she thwarted a burglary. I thought you'd be eager for her to move on."

He didn't get a chance to answer, assuming he could figure out an appropriate response, because Carson Ingalls was tapping on the board table again. The crowd quieted.

After thanking everyone present for their input, the board members debated among themselves. Although Alice opposed the destruction of the cottage, she was concerned about the cost of legal action. In addition to paying an attorney to file the suit, the residents might be on the hook for even more if Sherry, whose name was listed as the property owner, sued *them* in return.

After further discussion, the board agreed to draft a letter asking the city council to designate the cottage as a historic landmark and ban its destruction. Otherwise, however, there would be no legal intervention.

Sherry beamed. Around the room, some residents scowled while others nodded. Oliver was grateful that the group appeared to accept the decision without rising up in open revolt.

He'd been worried that they might target him with their anger. He still had to do business among these folks.

Chairs scraped back and papers rustled. People drifted out. To Oliver's annoyance, Brooke had resumed her conversation with Bart. How much could they find to say about beans and tomatoes?

"We appreciate your help." Winston clapped Oliver on the shoulder, pulling his attention back to his companions. "Listen, I'm afraid I'll be out of town Tuesday. Rather than postpone our meeting, why don't we talk now?"

Oliver hesitated. He'd intended to set aside an hour or

so the following day to prepare his points. However, he couldn't afford to let this opening pass. "Sure."

Sherry, who'd arrived in a separate car, said her farewells, and the men strolled to the half-empty far end of the parking lot for privacy. "What's on your mind?" Winston asked.

Oliver, who'd been hurriedly organizing his ideas, tuned out the background noise from clubhouse and automobiles. "As I've mentioned, I want very much to invest in the Santa Martina project. A million dollars, though... I can't swing that right now. Especially since the fire at my condo."

Winston gave a start. He didn't seem pleased, although it was hard to read his reaction. "Then what's this conversation about?"

"I'd love to be involved in some other capacity. I have lots of ideas for promotion and marketing." Pushing on, Oliver sketched out a few of them.

Winston listened with cool reserve, the spotty lighting darkening his blond hair and emphasizing the hollows in his cheeks. Until now, Winston had seemed young for his thirty-eight years. Tonight, however, his responsibilities seemed to weigh heavily on him.

At last the financier spoke. "Those are good ideas. Some of them I'd considered already, but not all."

"Publicizing them might help sell the remaining investment shares," Oliver added.

"As it happens, the response was so good I'm afraid I may have undervalued them. We should be sold out soon."

Disappointment shot through Oliver. Perhaps his contribution wasn't needed, after all.

"On the plus side," the developer continued, "I've been

thinking you'd be a good man to bring on board. I like to have forward thinkers on my staff."

Was Winston offering him a job? While Oliver wasn't sure how such a move would affect his real-estate business or his long-term plans, he'd love the challenge. "You mean…?"

"Two weeks ago, our vice president of international development suffered a heart attack. He may have to retire," Winston continued. "We've been keeping the whole thing under wraps until we learn more about his condition. In the interim, the board has asked me to identify the right replacement, should the position open up."

Oliver's heart raced. Vice president of international development! What a coup. He had figured he'd lost any such opportunity when he'd abandoned his dream of earning a masters degree in business because he'd been unwilling to take on a crushing load of student loans.

"There's one other issue." Winston folded his arms. "I don't have to tell you how much perceptions count. Our investors will feel a lot more confident if they see that you believe in the project enough to invest your own money. There'll be profit sharing for top execs, so you should net a quick return."

"I can't raise a million dollars." It killed Oliver to admit it.

Winston appeared to assess him. "You're a sharp guy and I believe in you. Under the circumstances, I can justify offering you a special arrangement. Can you raise half a million?"

Oliver performed some calculations. He refused to sell all three of his properties—owning real estate was too fundamental to his portfolio. But he could part with the beach bungalow. And that left…his business.

Years of hard work, gone. Still, he wouldn't have time to run it with this new job. Was he prepared to take such a risk?

"I'll have to crunch some numbers," he told Winston. "When do you need an answer?"

"I don't mean to rush you," came the answer. "As I told you, we're not a hundred percent sure our veep is leaving. But if he does, my board will insist on filling the position fast."

"Finding a buyer for my business could take months."

Winston didn't look pleased. "Then you'll have to borrow against it."

A scary thought. Still, Oliver had borrowed money to open his office in the first place—a debt he'd long ago repaid. "I'll do my best."

"So will I." The blond man's voice rang with assurance. "You proceed full speed ahead, and if that post opens up I'll give you first crack at it."

"Great." They shook hands.

Excitement edged with nervousness tingled through Oliver as Winston departed. A huge step…a big gamble… but what a break! He might never again get such an opportunity to join a major enterprise.

About to walk home, Oliver heard a familiar voice on the sidewalk ahead. Brooke.

"Tomorrow would be great," she told Bart as the pair ambled along, his rangy frame towering over her. Neither appeared to notice Oliver.

Tomorrow would be great for what?

"You okay walking back?" Bart asked. "I've got my car here. I was heading for a late Bible-study session at my church, but I can drop you at your house."

"Don't bother," Oliver called across the blacktop. "I'm here."

"Great!" With a casual wave, Bart slid into a dented pickup.

Good riddance. Dismayed at his own behavior, since he'd always gotten along fine with the gardener, Oliver caught up with Brooke.

"Hey," she greeted him. "Pleased with how things turned out?"

"Ecstatic."

Now she was falling behind. "Slow down, would you?"

"Sorry." He adjusted his pace.

How enjoyable to walk home together, Oliver thought, his spirits calming down. Brooke looked darling in her long skirt and embroidered blouse. And he had her all to himself.

Not for much longer, though. With luck, he'd soon be off to the Caribbean, or perhaps Paris or Tokyo, where Winston's company also had offices.

That would leave Bart or any other guy on her list a clear field with Brooke. Oliver's stomach clenched. Yet, much as he hated thinking about her with another man, he had an obligation to keep her safe. The best way to do that, like it or not, was to help her find Mr. Right.

Grimly, Oliver made up his mind to do just that.

Chapter Ten

Absorbed in planning the layout of her future garden, Brooke didn't register the brisk temperature of the evening air until Oliver said to her, "If you're cold, I'd be happy to lend you my jacket."

Much as she relished the prospect of wrapping herself in the jacket, which was steeped in his scent, she couldn't accept. "No, thanks."

"You might catch a chill." He kept to the street side of the sidewalk in the old-fashioned way of a gentleman.

Considering the fact that he'd more or less ignored her all evening, this new attentiveness enveloped her with its warmth. Not that she needed any extra warming up.

"Apparently, pregnant women are like radiators," she said. "I'm sure I've raised the temperature in Brea by a couple of degrees just being out here." They turned onto a side street. Lights shone from windows and the soaring voice of a soprano wafted from one of the houses.

"I thought it was older women who had hot flashes," Oliver said.

"Flashes? I'm permanently set on high."

He chuckled. "I'll lower the thermostat then, and save a fortune."

"Be my guest." She hadn't adjusted the temperature since she'd moved in. That might be because she hadn't figured out where the thermostat was yet.

She spoke again half a block later. "What's on your mind?"

"The usual."

She doubted that, after the way he'd gone off with that financier. "Oh, come on. What were you and Winston talking about?"

Oliver took a deep breath. "His resort project, of course."

"I thought you weren't going to invest in it." She hoped that was still the case. Seeing him with Winston and Sherry had disturbed her.

"That might change."

"Are you sure you want to do that? He seems slippery to me." Still, her dislike of the man might stem in part from his association with Sherry. What had the woman been thinking, to stand up and sneer at the other residents for living in ordinary homes? And then she'd seemed shocked by their response.

In the moonlight Oliver frowned. "The man's a high-level salesman. Maybe that's why he comes across as glib. I'm sure plenty of people think *I'm* slippery."

"Not me."

"Well, thanks." They swung onto Crestridge Road, which abutted their street. "There's a possibility I may go to work for Winston's company. Please don't mention this to anyone—including Renée. It's very preliminary."

"Okay. But I don't understand. How can you work for him and run your own business?"

"I can't. I'd have to sell it and relocate."

The news jolted her. "You're leaving?"

"It's all speculation at this point."

With an effort she reined in her anxiety. Very preliminary, he'd said. Maybe it wouldn't happen at all.

Please let him stay.

"What are you and Bart planning to do tomorrow?" he
asked.

She snapped back to reality. A reality in which she had
to deal with her own situation, regardless of whether Oliver
stayed or went.

"He's coming over at lunchtime to advise me on planting a garden." But if Oliver was departing… "If I won't
be around long enough to harvest a garden, I guess I should
cancel our meeting."

"Don't worry," he said. "For one thing, my plans are up
in the air."

"What's the other thing?"

"Beg pardon?"

"You said, 'For one thing,' so…"

"Renée mentioned Bart's on your husband list. Don't
want to discourage him, right?"

"You're going along with the whole Mr. Right thing?"
Despite Oliver's acquiescence, she'd received the impression he considered the whole project pretty lame. And
judging by the way he'd glowered at Bart, she wondered
if he might not be feeling the pricks of jealousy.

Of course, that was probably just wishful thinking on
her part.

"It's crazy. Still, who knows? You're attractive, and
some men do long to be fathers."

"How about you?" The question popped out unpre-
meditated.

"Me?"

"I don't mean in my particular case," she hurried to explain. "I mean, in general."

"Me, a dad? I don't think so."

Disappointment tightened her throat. Okay, she'd been foolish to daydream about him even in passing, but she had. Once or twice. "You dislike kids?"

"They're great for other people," Oliver said. "Just not for me."

"That's the sum total of your views on fatherhood?"

"Pretty much." He cleared his throat. "So, back to Bart. Since I agreed to check out your candidates, I guess I'd better join the two of you tomorrow."

"Fine with me." Brooke would enjoy his company, and after all, the yard *did* belong to him. Still, as far as rating Bart's qualifications for the altar, Brooke suspected Oliver's involvement might be counterproductive.

Earlier in the evening she'd been getting along fine with Bart, until she'd spotted Oliver across the room and compared them. The other man lacked Oliver's spark and wit, not to mention his easy masculine grace.

She must be losing her mind. How could she have developed a fondness for a man she'd long dismissed as arrogant and pigheaded?

He *was* arrogant and pigheaded. But she liked him, anyway. So much for leading with her brain.

"Who else is on the list?" he probed.

"The Foxes mentioned a few other guys. I'll look into them." Another name popped up. "Then there's Sean Sawyer."

"And he is…?"

"Jane's partner."

"You're considering romancing your doctor?" he asked.

"I haven't met him yet," Brooke admitted. "I found a photo online, and he's not bad-looking." In truth, the shot made him look like a movie star. Maybe the photographer had airbrushed it.

"An ob-gyn? I'll bet he's married."

"Not according to Jane." Her new friend had seemed amazed that a world full of women had missed this treasure. "She raves about the man."

"Must be something wrong with him. Women line up to marry handsome doctors. He must have some fatal flaw."

"Your neighbor claims he's wonderful." Jane hadn't fallen for him, though, Brooke noted.

Oliver's eyes narrowed. "When are you seeing him?"

She thought for a moment. "Wednesday at, um, five-fifteen."

At the top of Harmony Road, they turned, passing Lois and Sarah Oldham's house on the corner. "I'll join you," he announced.

Oliver wanted to go to the doctor with her? That ought to be interesting. Brooke tried to picture him seated in a waiting room full of big-bellied women and baby magazines. "Are you sure?"

"Positive. I promised to screen your candidates, didn't I? Now, who else did you say is on the list?"

"Just the ones I don't know much about." Wait—another name was circling for a landing. "Oh, yeah. Your cousin Rafe."

He stumbled and broke stride. They'd reached his house, Brooke realized. "You're kidding!"

"He's not bad-looking," she pointed out. "Since he's raising a niece and nephew who aren't even his own children, why should he object to mine?"

"He's got a stubborn streak and his relationships with women never last more than a few months." Ascending the porch, Oliver produced a key.

"He's *your* cousin. How bad can he be?"

For a moment, Oliver seemed to be searching for an argument. Then his lips twitched. "That sounds like a compliment."

"I guess it was."

"Thanks." He ushered her inside. "Sorry, but I've got some numbers to crunch."

For Winston. Again she got a bad feeling. But she had no right to interfere. "Crunch away."

She hurried past him to assess the contents of the refrigerator. As usual these days, she was starving.

HALF A MILLION DOLLARS was less than the cost of an average house in Orange County. Yet it seemed like a fortune to the son of a warehouseman and a homemaker. And the grandson of Mexican farmworkers on his mother's side.

Still, how could he resist the opportunity of a lifetime?

By midmorning on Monday, Oliver had finished poring over his profit-and-loss statements, trying to estimate the value of his brokerage. Then he called in his top agent, Sanford "Sandy" Rivers, to ask whether he might be interested in buying the business.

"Wow, you bet!" Sandy's pudgy face radiated enthusiasm. "What kind of price are we talking about?" With his soft features and thinning hair, he projected an everyman image customers related to. They also seemed to sense that he was honest, hard-working and knowledgeable.

Oliver named a sum.

"That's a bit steep for my wallet. Can I have some time to review it?" Sandy asked.

"Would a few days be enough?"

"I'll get right on it."

Oliver had a lot of respect for the go-getter. He suspected Sandy would find a way to come up with the money.

It was lunchtime. He'd better get a move on or he'd miss Bart's visit.

At home he found the two of them in the backyard. In the sunshine Brooke had an earthy, appealing glow. He didn't see how Bart could resist her. And yet, the man seemed more interested in evaluating the weedy patch of ground he and Brooke were examining. "Plants require at least six to eight hours of sunshine, which this ought to provide. The soil looks pretty bad, though."

"The former tenants weren't exactly candidates for a feature on beautiful homes and gardens," Oliver told him. "*Everything* deteriorated while they were here."

"Oh, this doesn't look bad for a rental. It has possibilities."

"Isn't that a euphemism for 'It's ugly as sin?'" Oliver joked.

Most of the grassy area was flat, except for a slope that was covered in ice plants at the back. A perimeter block wall, topped on one side with a spray of the Oldhams' golden roses and on the other by Jane McKay's bougainvillea, provided privacy.

"I love it," Brooke declared. "All of it." Returning her attention to Bart, she asked, "What should we do about the soil?"

He droned on about compost and organic material, like a full-fledged hippie farmer. If he and Brooke married, no doubt they'd eat lentils for dinner every night and keep chickens and cows in the garage.

Chiding himself for his ill humor, Oliver conceded that Brooke would look pretty cute milking a cow. And as for Bart, he'd cut a fine figure riding a tractor.

Preferably off into the sunset.

In response to a question that Oliver had missed, their guest said, "Corn requires a lot of space for a small yield. I'd suggest sticking to heavy producers like tomatoes and zucchini. If you decide to grow beans, the pole variety bears more fruit."

"Fruit?" Oliver repeated absentmindedly.

"In the technical sense," Bart confirmed. "If you eat the plant, like celery or carrots, that's a vegetable. If you harvest a seed-producing body—"

"Thanks for the botany lesson." Tired of wasting time, Oliver went straight to the point. "How do you feel about kids?"

"Kids?" repeated Bart.

Brooke folded her arms in obvious disapproval of his blunt tactics. Well, Oliver didn't have all day. "I imagine someone committed to nature would be eager to have children."

Bart scratched his ear. "I consider plants my children. Adding to the earth's overpopulation isn't my style."

"That's what you think about when you see kids—overpopulation?" Brooke asked in disbelief.

"Maybe someday I'll look back and regret not having any," Bart mused. "But I believe people should live by their beliefs. Besides, I'm pretty happy living alone. Any more questions?"

"What about lettuce?"

Oliver didn't get her point. She wasn't giving birth to a head of iceberg, was she?

Then he realized she'd returned to the subject of gardening. Bart had grasped the point at once. "It's a cool-weather crop, but it should do well. Be sure to position the low-growing plants where the taller ones won't shade them."

Now that they'd settled the matter of the gardener's suitability—or lack thereof—Oliver tuned out the rest of the man's words. Citing his short lunch break as an excuse, he left the pair alone and went inside for a sandwich.

A short while later Brooke joined him in the kitchen. "That's your idea of screening for husband material? Why don't you just hit 'em on the head with a sledgehammer?"

Oliver swallowed. "How would that help?"

"You're hopeless."

"Is he gone?"

"Yes." Brooke retrieved a jar of peanut butter. "I'm reconsidering letting you go to the doctor with me."

"Why?"

"Because I refuse to let you insult him. Besides, I can judge his character for myself," she said. "I mean, he's a doctor, for heaven's sake!"

"Just because he's an obstetrician, it doesn't mean he's dying to have children. With you or anybody else."

"And you're just the man to ask him? Straight out and in the most embarrassing manner possible?" She spread some peanut butter on a whole-wheat tortilla. Oliver watched, fascinated. Man, that looked way better than his turkey cold cuts.

"Somebody has to."

After adding a long slice of banana, she rolled the whole thing into a flute.

"Fix me one?"

She thrust it at him and set to work on a second. "I'm serious. That was rude."

"I apologize if I hurt your feelings."

"Not mine. His!" She formed another flute.

"I *am* going to the doctor with you," Oliver insisted, postponing his first bite in case his mouth got stuck shut. "You can't be objective when he's running his hands all over you."

"It isn't like that."

"How do you know? Maybe he's got the world's hottest bedside manner."

"You're projecting your own out-of-control libido. If you find my pregnant body so irresistible, you should at least try to stay on my good side."

About to respond smartly, Oliver decided to down a quick bite of the peanut butter, instead. Delicious. Sticky. A man couldn't get a word out for at least a minute.

He was still chewing when Brooke stalked out the room with her peanut-butter wrap and a glass of milk in hand. Which was just as well, because what could he say that wouldn't land him in even more trouble?

EVEN THOUGH SHE'D AGREED to it, Brooke had second thoughts about bringing Oliver to the clinic on Wednesday. And third and fourth thoughts.

He'd had some nerve implying that Dr. Sawyer might behave unprofessionally. Or that Brooke might be so overcome by the physician's charms that lust would seize her right there on the examining table.

Still, Oliver appeared to be behaving as they sat on a couch awaiting their turn. He'd brought along a copy of *Forbes* magazine, which spared him from reading the baby and maternity periodicals scattered about. The only other patient in the waiting room was a woman in her thirties, dressed in an expensive, well-tailored maternity outfit.

She must have planned for this pregnancy, Brooke thought, longed for it and poured tons of money into it. Her baby would have the best of everything.

Leafing through a magazine, Brooke studied the ads for baby furniture with growing alarm. How could she ever afford all the things she was going to need? Diapers, baby clothes, day care…

No sense panicking. Someone or something would turn up.

And if it doesn't?

She'd worry about that later. Her anxiety would pass soon enough. Yet an unfamiliar twist of fear continued to churn in her stomach.

After half an hour, Oliver approached the receptionist's desk and then reported back that the doctor was running late due to an emergency. "I explained we're in a bit of a hurry. I have an appointment at seven-thirty tonight."

It wasn't even six o'clock yet. "I can't imagine the doctor taking *that* long."

A nurse emerged through an inner door. "Brooke Bernard?"

She lurched to her feet. In her haste, she lost her balance and swayed until Oliver caught her arm.

His face dipped close to hers. Mmm, that fresh, masculine scent. She clung for a moment before straightening up.

"You okay?" he murmured.

"Yup. Thanks." All the same, she still held on to his arm as they followed the nurse.

Brooke had pictured Oliver there on the sidelines while

she exchanged bright, baby-related banter with a handsome man in a white coat. Despite their joking about the exam, she hadn't given much thought to the fact that medical visits involved getting weighed, providing blood and other specimens and then…

The nurse handed her a scanty hospital gown and gave her instructions to disrobe. "Dr. Sawyer usually meets with his patients in his office before doing the pelvic exam, but your husband said you're in a hurry."

"He's not my husband."

"I'm sorry." She smiled. "I meant, the *father* said you're in a hurry. Press this button on the wall to notify us when you're ready." Out she whisked.

The father. Brooke stole a glance at Oliver. A natural assumption, she supposed.

If he minded, he gave no sign. Instead, he indicated the gown. "Should I step out?"

"Darn right. And stay there until he's done looking up my…whatever." After a beat, she appended, "Please."

"Wait a minute." Oliver folded his arms. "You're willing to let this complete stranger, whom you're considering as marriage material, take a gander at…at your *whatever,* but you're excluding me, your faithful housemate?"

"Out!"

"Just asking," he said, and disappeared.

When she'd changed into the laughably inadequate gown, Brooke pressed the button and hopped onto the examining table, hugging her knees to her chest as she sat there. She wouldn't be able to sit in this position much longer, she realized as she felt the firm shape of her abdomen. She was already having difficulty finding a comfortable position for sleeping.

Glancing at a diagram on the wall of a baby inside its mother, she noticed how huge the woman's abdomen looked. Was *she* going to pooch out that far? Good heavens, how could she drive? How could she work?

Brooke concentrated on breathing steadily. It helped.

A knock preceded the entrance of… Was this *him?* Tousled hair, rough-hewn features, broad shoulders. "I'll bet you hear this a lot, but are you sure you aren't a movie star playing a doctor?" Brooke asked.

A laugh revealed teeth perfect enough to grace Dr. Salonica's window display. "I don't believe anyone's ever put it that way." He extended a hand. "I'm Sean Sawyer."

She shook, finding his grip firm and reassuring. "Brooke Bernard. We have a lot in common."

"Our friendship with Jane?"

"That, and double initials," she said. "SS, meet BB."

Another chuckle. "My pleasure."

She *liked* this guy. Of course, she suspected that every woman who crossed his path probably fell for him, yet according to Jane, he was still looking for the woman of his dreams.

With luck, she might just be sitting right here in front of him.

Chapter Eleven

Oliver grimaced as he listened to the merry interplay of voices from behind the closed door. Doctors already had a big advantage over the rest of the male species. It seemed unreasonable for this Sawyer fellow to also come equipped with great looks and the build of an athlete.

It wasn't hard to imagine the scene in there. Brooke practically naked, her cute face beaming up at him. How could any guy resist that?

Oliver focused on the fact that he *wanted* Brooke to marry this man. He ought to be grateful they'd formed an instant bond.

Grateful? He ached to chase the presumptuous fellow back to whatever football field he'd come from.

In the corridor the nurse paused beside him. "Excuse me, sir. Are you feeling light-headed?"

"What? No."

"You look kind of pale."

With anger, maybe. "Lack of sun."

She patted his arm as if he'd said something endearing. Or endearingly childish. "If things start spinning, don't be afraid to sit on the floor." When he failed to respond, she added, "We're used to it. Some fathers experience symptoms of pregnancy right along with their wi...significant others."

That was news to him. "Do they swell up, too?"

"Sometimes," she said. "They gain weight, experience morning sickness, the whole shebang. It's called Couvade syndrome."

"Is there a cure?"

"Childbirth."

How strange. "Men have babies?"

"I meant the mother's childbirth."

"Interesting." As the woman went about her duties, Oliver doubted he had a problem with his hormones. He'd already made his diagnosis.

Jealousy.

No! He meant protectiveness.

He endorsed the notion of Brooke finding a nice guy to coddle her and the baby. A good friend. A pal. Not someone she'd fall for hook, line and sinker, because then she'd end up with another broken heart.

The examining-room door opened. "Your lady's ready for you to join us," announced the suave Dr. Sawyer. He didn't offer to shake hands, since he'd already done that once and introduced himself on the way in.

"Great."

Oliver found Brooke sitting on the examining table, wrapped in a paper-towel-size garment and clutching a couple of brochures. Her eyes were shining.

Straight at the doctor.

"What're those?" Oliver indicated the booklets.

"Information about nutrition and childbirth classes. Doesn't that sound like fun?"

Lots of fun, probably involving plenty of doctor visits. "For thousands of years, women popped out their babies in fields," Oliver grumbled.

"And died during childbirth."

"Today, we have great success at treating complications during pregnancy," Dr. Sawyer told them. "Any questions?"

Neither of them could think of any.

"Then perhaps we should discuss sex," the physician said.

Oliver's jaw didn't just drop, it plummeted. "Excuse me?"

"This is the part that interests dads." The doctor continued. "As long as there are no problems such as bleeding, sex is fine throughout pregnancy. The baby's well cushioned, and for some women sex feels especially good."

This was *way* more than Oliver wished to discuss with this particular expert. "Fine. Great." *As long as the sex doesn't involve you.*

"Any other questions before we listen to the heartbeat?"

Oliver glanced at his watch. Six-thirty-five. "Will that take long?" Darn it, he didn't mean to be callous. "It's just that I have a listing appointment in an hour."

"Most people get excited about hearing their child's heartbeat."

Brooke spoke up. "Oliver isn't excited because the baby isn't real to him yet."

"Well, let's make it real. I'll just fetch some equipment." With those words, Dr. Sawyer strode into the hall.

Brooke sighed. A happy sigh, Oliver gathered from her radiant expression. "In a good mood?"

"Isn't he fabulous?" she gushed. "No wonder Jane adores him. I didn't even mind the exam."

Oliver flexed his hands, suffering an inexplicable urge to form them into fists. How strange. He ought to be overjoyed for her, assuming the doctor was also attracted to her.

And how could he help it?

Dr. Sawyer returned, pushing a cart of electronic equipment. "I was considering doing an ultrasound, anyway, to confirm your dates. Normally I wouldn't have time, but Ms. Bernard's my last patient of the day."

He acted cheerful about this imposition on his schedule. Didn't the fellow ever get cranky? Maybe he wasn't human, Oliver reflected darkly. Maybe someone had developed perfect robot doctors, and Sean Sawyer was the prototype.

The doctor misunderstood his scowl. "Don't worry, Dad. We'll get you out of here in plenty of time."

"Thanks." No matter how long this took, Oliver wasn't leaving Brooke alone here with a gorgeous robot.

Once she bared her rounded midsection, the physician spread gel and applied a paddle device. She seemed so deep under this guy's spell that she'd forgotten Oliver existed.

Then her hand slid into his, small and trusting. Embarrassed by his foolish thoughts, he focused on the swirling black-and-white images that appeared on the computer screen.

A pulsing dot maintained a steady rhythm. "What's that?"

"The heart," Dr. Sawyer said.

Oliver stared, fascinated. A miniature beating heart. How amazing.

"Isn't it too quick?" Brooke asked.

"Babies' hearts beat faster than ours. Okay, here we go. There's the head and shoulders. I can make out an arm...."

Oliver stared as the shape of the baby emerged. With Brooke barely showing, he hadn't imagined her baby could be so fully formed. That was a little person in there, with eyes and ears and hands and feet. Could it hear them talking? Was it feeling the pressure as the fluid shifted around it?

"Let's take some pictures." Pausing the movements of the paddle, the doctor clicked the computer. "I might be able to guess at the gender, if you're curious about that."

Until this moment, Oliver *hadn't* been. Now he wondered if it might be a little girl like Brooke, or a boy like... Never mind. "Doesn't matter."

"To me, either," she said.

"From the size, I'd estimate you're three months along. That puts the due date around October second." More clicking.

"October second," she repeated in wonder.

Where would Oliver be then? Jetting around the globe pursuing investment possibilities? Striding across the resort construction site with Winston?

He knew where the good doctor would be. In the delivery room, beaming at Brooke as he held the baby in his arms. And she'd beam right back. Well, maybe not at first. There might be a little screaming and sweating along the way, but she'd look adorable doing it.

"You must love your job," she was saying.

"It's a kick. And this is the best part, seeing a baby for the first time." Removing the paddle, the physician wiped the goo from her stomach.

"Did you always plan to be an obstetrician?"

"Not until I was halfway through medical school. I just wanted to help people."

Of course he did. They programmed him to say that. Unfair, Oliver corrected. The guy was obviously sincere.

"Someday, when I've paid off my student loans, I'm going to move to a Third World country where women receive little prenatal care," the doctor continued. "Think how much good I could do."

"Wow." Brooke regarded him as if he'd just sprouted angel wings.

"I doubt that'll happen before October, though," he added with a teasing smile.

"I hope not!"

This cloying exchange was annoying the heck out of Oliver. "If we're done here…"

"Let me print a couple of shots. You can take your baby's first picture home with you." Dr. Sawyer pressed a button. Out of the printer purred two black-and-white images.

Brooke regarded them with delight. "These are breathtaking."

Yes, they were. Studying the baby's image, Oliver nodded, his throat too tight for speech.

"Nice to meet you both." After handshakes all around, the world's most ideal bachelor departed.

Brooke shooed Oliver out while she got dressed. Alone in the corridor, he phoned to confirm his seven-thirty appointment.

"Oh, gosh, I meant to call you," the woman said. "We signed yesterday with my brother-in-law. Mostly he sells washers and dryers for a living. He has a real-estate license, but he doesn't know much about multiple listings or how to get the house ready for buyers. Would you mind stopping by our place and answering some questions?"

Oh, sure, I love working for free. Instead, Oliver gave her a website address where she could find basic information for sellers.

"Thanks. This is terrific." Ms. Clueless rang off.

Although disappointed at losing a chance to earn thousands of dollars in commission, Oliver shrugged. Par for the course.

Brooke reappeared, dressed again. "Wasn't that unbelievable?" she said, as they went out of the clinic and into the twilight.

"Quite an experience." One that had changed Oliver's perceptions, he admitted to himself. Now he felt compelled to shield Brooke *and* that little person from everything life might throw their way. "You were right. The baby didn't seem real to me till now."

"I guess it wasn't completely real to me, either," she responded thoughtfully.

Much as he hated to ask, Oliver had to phrase the question. "Do you think Dr. Sawyer might be Mr. Right?"

Brooke clicked open her car door. They'd arrived separately, since Oliver had expected to go from the doctor's visit to his appointment. "He's *too* perfect. Who wants to live with Albert Schweitzer day in and day out?"

He was glad to hear it. Maybe a little too glad. After all, she *did* need a husband. "You're sure? You seemed taken with him."

"You're the one whose hand I wanted to hold."

A tingle of excitement defied his common sense. He wanted to hold *her* hand, too. Over dinner.

"My appointment canceled," he said. "Let me take you out to eat."

"That would be great."

The ringing of his cell phone forestalled further discussion. "Hang on," Oliver said. "Let me get this."

And for the first time ever, he hoped that it *wasn't* someone calling to list a house.

SITTING BEHIND the wheel, Brooke studied the images of her baby while Oliver chatted with his caller. By the beginning of October, this tiny creature was going to be a full-fledged child.

She found the prospect exhilarating. And extremely scary.

If only she had someone like Oliver by her side. A guy to have fun with and cook for. A man who always told the truth, who never cheated or disappeared.

But Oliver *did* plan to disappear. What was the big deal about some Caribbean resort? Southern California had plenty of tourist attractions. Surely he could find similar business opportunities in this area.

Her grip on the pictures tightened, and only with an effort did Brooke manage to stop herself from crumpling them. Was she actually fantasizing about Oliver?

This had to stop. Right here, right now.

The object of her dismay spoke to her through the car window. "That was Rafe. He's got an emergency at the garage and he asked if we could pick up his kids at day care. I'm afraid we'll have to change our plans for dinner."

Her stomach rumbled. *Gee, thanks, Rafe.* "What kind of emergency can there be at a garage?" A car wasn't going to bleed to death if you delayed treatment overnight.

"He gave a client his word that he'd finish a major job

by this evening. He's running behind because of another problem that cropped up." Oliver shook his head. "You're not going to believe what it was."

Her interest stirred. "Tell me."

"Sherry LaSalle was driving by his place when her car conked out. She insisted he fix it on the spot. Threw a hissy fit, according to Rafe. You should have heard him carrying on about the nerve of the woman. Anyway, he was able to replace the broken part in a hurry, but he warned her it'll break down again if she doesn't deal with the underlying problem. She paced the waiting room the entire time, threw her credit card at him and then drove off without even saying a thank you."

"How rude." Brooke sympathized both with Rafe *and* the kids. "Those little tykes are still at day care? They must be starving."

"How about if I pick up a pizza and you collect Juan and Sofia? That way we can still eat."

A reasonable compromise. "Great."

He gave her the address—eleven Harmony Road, just down the street from his house. She'd been curious to see the day-care center, anyway.

"They're both four, by the way. Twins," Oliver noted. "And thanks. You're a good sport."

"I love being around kids." What she lacked in experience she could always make up for in enthusiasm, Brooke thought as she drove away.

A few minutes later, however, she didn't feel quite so certain of that. Maryam Hughes, a graceful woman in her forties, whose silver necklace bore a dramatic African-style design, stood beside her in a den littered with torn paper, crumpled coloring books and scattered crayons.

A dark-haired boy and girl sat sullenly on a sofa, their feet dangling. "I sent my son and daughter to their rooms," Maryam said. "They're close to the same age and usually the four of them get along."

Brooke regarded the scene in dismay. She would never have dreamed of making such a mess at that age. "What was the fight about?"

"They were all just tired. Let's go fetch their jackets." The day-care provider led her into a side room. "After their parents died last summer, Juan and Sofia seemed kind of stunned at first. Now the loss seems to be sinking in and they're becoming a real handful."

"That must be tough on everyone." Those two needed a mother. Could that person be Brooke?

She had a lot of love to share. And their father did meet her qualifications: he was available, he was willing to be a parent and he was financially solvent. Too bad he reminded her so much of his cousin without actually *being* Oliver.

She and the children set off on foot. She'd left her car at Oliver's, since she lacked children's car seats. One more thing she'd have to buy.

"We live there." Sofia pointed to a house across the street.

"The witch owns *that* house." Juan indicated Sherry's cottage.

"That's what your uncle calls her?"

"Yeah," they said in chorus.

That ought to improve neighborly relations, Brooke mused.

Oliver hadn't returned yet. The children soon tired of exploring and they refused Brooke's invitation to play a game, so she found an episode of *Sesame Street* on TV. She'd always sworn never to use television as a babysitter, and here she was doing it right off the bat.

The kids bounced on the sofa, poking each other until another battle seemed imminent. Keeping an eye on them from the kitchen, Brooke dialed Renée and sketched out the situation. "What should I do?"

"You're asking me?" her friend demanded in disbelief. "I'm the antimom."

High heels. Long blond hair. Weekends in Vegas. Brooke sighed. "Never mind."

"So how's it going with your roomie?" her friend asked before she could hang up.

"Can you believe he accompanied me to the doctor?" Seeing that the twins had become absorbed in Bert and Ernie's antics, Brooke took a minute to describe the visit. "He acted almost jealous of Dr. Sawyer. Isn't that strange?"

"No," Renée said. "He likes you."

"Not the way he liked *you.*"

"Get real. You and Oliver generate more sparks than he and I ever did."

The statement baffled Brooke. How could anyone compare *her* to the drop-dead-gorgeous hairdresser? "You're joking."

"No."

"I'm so sorry!"

"Don't be," her friend advised. "In fact, I'm rooting for you guys."

"There's no chance of…" A screech from the den interrupted Brooke. "Sorry. Have to go stop a murder."

Finding the twins more agitated than ever, Brooke darted into her room and returned with the panda, purple bear and green rabbit that Kevin had given her. "You can each pick one of these to take home," she told them. "But if you fight any more, the deal's off."

Juan studied her in disbelief. "Honest? We can keep them?"

"Honest." To forestall another squabble, she said, "Ladies first."

"The bunny," Sofia decided.

For once, her brother didn't object. "The panda's *way* better."

Brooke handed them over gladly, and only then realized her actions constituted bribery. That was another thing she'd sworn never to resort to.

Being a mom was far more complicated in reality than in theory.

She sat between the kids and they all watched Big Bird prance around on the screen. Soon Sofia's head drooped against one shoulder, followed on the other side by Juan's. Sleepy, they were so darling that Brooke forgave their earlier misbehavior.

Luckily the growling of her stomach didn't disturb them. But where the heck was Oliver?

Chapter Twelve

As Oliver angled his way into the house balancing two large pizzas and his laptop case, he half expected to receive a scolding. It wasn't his fault that a deliveryman at the pizza place had sped off with his order by mistake. By the time anyone noticed the error it had been too late to call the guy back from his other deliveries, so they had to bake new ones.

The chatter of a children's TV program greeted him. From behind, he spotted Brooke on the sofa. Where were the kids?

He stepped right into the room. Ah, there they were, on either side of Brooke, their heads nestled into her sides. Both were dozing.

What an endearing picture. His imagination flashed forward six months or so. She'd be holding her own baby as she tilted her head and smiled sleepily up at…

Not him.

Why not him?

Lots of reasons.

"There you are," Brooke murmured.

"Sorry I'm late. The pizzeria screwed up." He kept his tone soft to avoid waking the twins. "Your line was busy."

"I must have been talking to Renée."

Beside her, Juan suddenly sat bolt upright. "Pizza!" His sister stirred, sniffed and joined him in a mad dash to the kitchen. So much for letting them doze while the adults enjoyed a bit of quiet.

Oliver forgot his pique as the kids dug in to their supper. Pepperoni proved a favorite with the four-year-olds, while Brooke preferred the veggie special. Happy chatter filled the kitchen.

Oliver wished that dinners had been this relaxed when he was growing up. In a way, experiencing mealtime with these two children dispelled some of his unpleasant associations. What an intriguing notion, that he might erase old beliefs caused by his parents' inadequacies in the raising of his own family.

Yeah, well, this *wasn't* his own family and a single dinner did not a lifetime make. Still, Oliver thought maybe he got a glimmer of why some men might be eager to have kids.

As they were finishing, Rafe arrived, reeking of motor oil, despite having made obvious efforts to clean up. The children greeted him with shouts and hugs.

After things settled down, he gladly accepted an offer of food. "I can't tell you how much I appreciate you guys babysitting." He transferred several slices of pizza to his plate. "What I need is a nanny."

A mom would be better. Oliver braced for Brooke's reaction. Of all the men on her list, this man was far and away the best prospect.

She'd be a member of the family. Even if he worked overseas, he could see her on holidays and watch her baby grow up.

And then she'd go home with Rafe.

He almost resented his cousin for being so ideally suited. Any second now, Brooke was going to pipe up and offer her services.

"Have you thought about running an ad?" she asked, instead.

Using a subtle approach, Oliver presumed. A wise choice, or she might spook the guy.

Rafe took a bite of his pizza. "I don't like the idea of hiring a stranger. I've heard horror stories."

Oliver caught his breath, waiting for Brooke to finish refilling Sofia's glass with more milk and point out that *she* was no stranger. Instead, she said, "Some nannies have excellent recommendations. I believe there are special schools that train them."

"Yeah, but that kind gets hired away fast by couples with money. My niece and nephew have suffered enough losses already. Besides, they enjoy playing with the other kids at Mrs. Hughes's house, right?" He addressed this question to Juan.

"I hate them!"

Rafe stared at his nephew. "I thought their son was your best friend."

"They had a fight today," Brooke explained. "They'll forget all about it by tomorrow."

Sofia yawned.

Rafe checked the clock. Although it seemed early to Oliver, his cousin whooped, "Bedtime!" with vast relief. Within minutes he'd bundled the small pair out the door.

Oliver insisted Brooke rest while he cleaned up. "I've seen Juan and Sofia in action," he remarked as he worked. "You must have nerves of steel."

"They're just acting out. They still miss their parents." She set her bare feet on the chair Sofia had occupied. "I admire your cousin for adopting them."

"He's never been the daddy type." Oliver put the milk carton back in the fridge. "He adored his younger brother, though. Stepped right in when it became clear none of the other relatives could handle those kids."

"Good guy."

He decided to be blunt. "I'm surprised you didn't apply to be his nanny."

"I already have a job. With medical benefits."

"This one might have marital benefits."

"Can we *not* talk about my search for a husband?"

"Okay." Obviously, she'd decided against Rafe. Although he suspected she must be running out of names, Oliver felt she'd made a wise choice.

They relocated to the patio, sinking side by side onto a glider. From a nearby yard drifted the scent of grilling hamburgers, and the indistinct voices of unseen neighbors punctuated the evening like the twittering of birds.

Brooke stretched. "How come nobody else in the family wanted the twins? I should think there'd be grandparents leaping at the chance."

"Rafe's father is an invalid." Oliver slid an arm across the glider, cushioning Brooke's neck. "My aunt takes care of him and my grandma Corazon."

"That's a pretty name. It means *heart* in Spanish, doesn't it?" She curled against him, her heat more than compensating for the evening coolness.

"She and my grandfather were migrant workers from Mexico." Oliver rarely gave much thought to his background. Unlike Rafe, who was Hispanic on both sides,

Oliver's mother's Mexican heritage was balanced by his father's German and Scottish ancestry.

"Well, they're adorable children. They need a lot of attention, though."

"Then let's hope Rafe finds the perfect nanny." Yielding to impulse, he tugged Brooke onto his lap. She curled against him. "Comfy?"

"Mm-hmm." Her cheek grazed his chest.

Oliver felt more than comfy. Stimulated, in fact. Holding her might not be the wisest idea in the world, but he was damned if he intended to release her just now.

"How's the baby?" He stroked her stomach, keenly sensitive to her voluptuous roundness. "Can you feel her move?"

"It's too soon. And why do you believe it's a girl?"

"I never mentioned that I'm psychic?"

"If you were psychic, you'd have crossed those guys off my list from the start." If she continued rocking against him, Oliver was going to display an unmistakable masculine reaction.

Too late.

Hoping she wouldn't notice, he said, "I figured you'd be more convinced if you crossed them off yourself."

"More convinced of what?"

How was he supposed to give a rational answer with his body making inappropriate demands? And his brain replaying the doctor's advice about sex: *Fine throughout pregnancy... Feels especially good.*

For whom? The man or the woman or both?

He tried to force his mind onto a safe topic. Well, perhaps not safe, so much as calculated to kill his ardor. "You must have other guys you're checking out, right?"

"The Foxes mentioned a few. Thank goodness for the Internet." Her chest rose and fell as she drew a long breath. Against Oliver's best intentions, her breasts caught his attention. She had never looked more enticing.

Stop. Right now. "You searched them out, I gather."

"Thank goodness. The engineer looks like a white rat and the attorney has just announced his engagement. As for Josh's subcontractor, in my condition I can't handle the smell of paint."

"They put people's body odors on the Web?" That *was* a new service.

"No. He's a painting contractor. He *has* to reek."

"I see. All the same…" With Brooke shifting her weight against his sensitive core, Oliver lost focus. "Do you have to keep moving like that?"

"You seem to be enjoying it." She *had* noticed. "You know what we're long overdue for?"

"I'm afraid to guess."

"This." Tilting her face to his, she brushed his lips with hers.

The humming inside him swelled to a chorus. Framing her face between his hands, he slanted his mouth over hers.

He only meant to kiss her for a moment. Then her tongue teased at his teeth and her arms wound around him tight. When her breasts pressed into his chest, he groaned and pulled her closer.

Summoning the last shreds of his self-control, Oliver eased her away. "Brooke, you know where this is likely to lead."

"What's wrong with that?"

Everything. "First, your expectations." A sharp pain in his earlobe gave him a start. "You bit me!"

"I didn't mean to nip so hard. It was supposed to be a love nip." She rubbed his ear to lessen the pain. "I have no expectations. Haven't you heard of friends with benefits?"

A bad idea, in his opinion. Except that he couldn't seem to produce any reasons for why that should be so.

This growing desire wasn't merely the result of the persistent gentle chafing in his lap. At some level he'd been craving Brooke for…how long?

Ages.

She was much more than an attractive woman well suited for a passionate encounter. She'd become a friend, a sympathetic soul, someone with whom he felt truly intimate.

Again her mouth met his, this time with more insistence. He sank into the kiss, yielding to a swell of longing. When he drew her near, the beating of her heart echoed within him until they seemed to throb with a single rhythm.

To hell with expectations.

Oliver lifted her to her feet. Kissing and touching each other over and over, they made their way inside. Somehow, without any conscious thought on his part, they arrived in his bedroom.

The bedroom where he'd spent the past few nights tossing and turning. Dreaming about her and refusing to admit it afterward.

She laughed and teased as they removed each other's clothing. What a responsive woman, totally in the moment! The sight of her lush contours stripped away the last of Oliver's restraint.

When they fell across the bed, he found her just as eager as he was to join together in one soaring, intense moment.

BROOKE COULDN'T BELIEVE Oliver wanted her this much.
Every caress, every stroke touched her soul. She loved
feeling his hardness inside her as she ran her hands across
his naked back.

More, more, more.

A tide of pleasure swelled within her. When the wave
came, she rode it to the far side of the ocean and back again.

Instead of the gradual ebbing she'd anticipated, however, she caught another surge of desire. It rose higher and
higher, cresting with a force that obliterated the memory
of any other man and any other moment.

Oliver was crying out, groaning and plunging—had he experienced anything like this before? She hadn't, not remotely.

Finished, Brooke lay spent in his arms, cherishing the
sheen of his skin and the smell of their lovemaking. She
wished that the baby she was carrying belonged to him.

Don't you dare start weaving plans around him. They
were friends with benefits. That was what they'd both
agreed on, and she aimed to stick by her word.

Brooke sighed. Being honorable was such a burden.

"You okay?" Oliver stroked her hair.

She nearly purred like a kitten. "Better than okay. You?"

"Phenomenal." He sounded completely at peace.

Brooke snuggled closer. She had to face the truth, even
if she couldn't act on it. She'd fallen in love with Oliver.
No telling when or how it had happened, or whether she
could have prevented it.

What that meant for her future and for the baby, she had
no idea. But she had to acknowledge that it had now become impossible to find Mr. Right.

Because she'd already found him.

THREE DAYS LATER, on Saturday morning, Oliver made breakfast. Okay, what he actually made was a mess, but at least he *tried* to fix pancakes.

Touched by his efforts, Brooke finished preparing the batter and showed him how to drop spoonfuls of the mixture onto a hot skillet. "I thought you weren't keen on eating sit-down meals," she murmured as she stood on tiptoe to kiss his jaw.

He looped one arm around her with casual possessiveness. "I was a fat kid. That put me off eating."

"You?" Astonishing.

"Meals were stressful at our house. You could write a dissertation about the psychology of childhood obesity, I'm sure. Are these ready to flip?"

She checked the edges for browning and demonstrated her technique. Oliver botched a couple of flapjacks before mastering it.

"By the way, we're eating applesauce on these, instead of syrup," he informed her.

"You're kidding!" She glanced at the table. Sure enough, that was what he'd set out. "You don't have to worry about gaining weight in one meal."

"No, but *you* should watch your sugar intake," Oliver replied. "Taking care of the baby means taking care of your health."

"You're watching over my diet?"

"I'm watching over *you*."

Joy enveloped Brooke. Although they'd spent the past few nights sleeping curled together, Oliver had been absurdly busy during their waking hours. She'd craved this kind of tenderness, even if meant giving up syrup till October.

The rest of the weekend passed in a dream. Although

Oliver still had to work, they found time for dinner together and long, slow lovemaking in the evening.

On Monday afternoon Brooke sat daydreaming at the Smile Central reception desk. She felt aglow with the happiness of nurturing a new life and watching her friendship with Oliver blossom into something deeper. He had yet to put his feelings into words, but she could wait.

She smoothed down the maternity top she'd just bought. Her old clothes had become tight these past few days, and accepting the inevitable, she'd gone shopping with Jane.

The phone rang. An appointment needed to be rescheduled. Her back turned to the entrance, Brooke heard the chimes that marked a new arrival, but assumed Faye would greet the patient.

Finished with the call, she stood and stretched, then swung around. A tall, elegant woman stood there, staring at Brooke in astonishment.

"Oh, my God." Helen Salonica's voice rose to a shriek. "You're pregnant!"

The three adults in the waiting room—bored parents whose children were in being treated—perked up at the drama. As for Faye, she folded her arms as if to say she'd seen this coming.

Brooke braved herself for further histrionics. Instead of lashing out, however, the boss's wife appeared mesmerized by the telltale maternity bulge. Her mouth trembled and tears glittered in her eyes.

With a twist of guilt, Brooke realized what this pregnancy must mean to a woman who believed her husband was the father. She had invested her whole life in raising a family and sustaining a marriage that must now appear to be on the verge of destruction.

"It isn't his," Brooke told her.

"Oh, please. What kind of fool do you take me for?"

Footfalls approaching from the inner rooms silenced them both. Dr. Salonica took in the scene with a frown. "What's going on?"

"She's having a baby." Helen pointed a finger. "Fire her!"

A teenage client, emerging from the inner room just behind the doctor, regarded the older woman with disapproval. "It's illegal to discriminate against pregnant women. We learned that in life-science class. Plus, it's mean."

Instead of replying, Helen stood there with tears trickling down her cheeks. Embarrassed, the girl ducked past her.

"Let's take this in my office," the orthodontist said.

Helen shook her head. "We'll discuss it at home." Unable to squeeze out further words, she ran.

"Helen…" Her husband's attempt to stop her came too late. She was gone. His attention shifted to Brooke. "It's really true, then?"

No point in denying the obvious. "Yes."

"Could you possibly create any more trouble?" he muttered.

"You going to fire her?" Faye seemed almost gleeful. Until now, Brooke hadn't realized her fellow receptionist was the type of person who actually enjoyed someone else's misfortune.

"We'll talk about it tomorrow," muttered their boss.

After his wife spent the night grinding him down, while Brooke tossed and turned? She'd rather hear the worst now. "Oh, no, we won't. Let's get this over with."

Dr. Salonica registered the curious gazes of the waiting-room occupants. "Oh, all right," he said, and retreated to his office.

Following, Brooke confronted the portly, balding man for whom she'd worked the past two years. She liked this job, and she appreciated the orthodontist's good qualities, compared to the attributes of her previous bosses. One had been sarcastic and rude to the staff; another had lied to clients and overcharged them. Dr. Salonica might be high-handed on occasion, but at least he had a good heart.

"You're way overdue on telling your wife the truth about your arrangement with Kevin," she said. "You can't go on protecting him." *No matter what secrets he's hiding for you.*

"Speaking of Kevin, does he know about the pregnancy?"

"Not yet." An important thought occurred to her. "My medical benefits depend on this job. If you're giving me the sack, there'll be serious consequences for me."

The man rubbed his forehead. "I'm not firing you—that would be unfair. It would also convince Helen beyond any doubt that you and I have been up to something."

Concern for her employer tempered Brooke's sense of relief. "Please don't put off telling her," she urged. "I'd hate to see you end up in a messy divorce that hurts everybody."

"I have pressures you can't understand. There are financial issues…" He sighed. "Never mind that. You're right in one respect. I have to level with Helen about Kevin, and about a past…mistake…that he covered up for me."

"Good luck." She finally allowed herself to rejoice in her narrow escape. "I'm glad I still have a job."

He nodded. "Of course, I have to tell Kevin he's going to be a father."

In her naïveté, she'd imagined she could avoid that a while longer. Maybe forever. "He ought to take care of the kids he's already got."

"That isn't your problem. Or mine," her boss said. "I'd better give him a call before my wife blabs to *his* wife."

Brooke considered the possibility of calling Kevin first. What good would that do, though?

The sad part was that his wife would hear about the pregnancy, from Helen if not from him. Brooke hated hurting an innocent woman. "Is there any way we can keep this whole thing secret?"

The orthodontist shook his head. "Word's probably all over town already."

"Brea isn't *that* small."

"You'd be surprised." He shrugged. "I'll see you tomorrow."

Grateful she still had a job, Brooke reentered the now empty waiting area, collected her purse and headed to Oliver's offices. Perhaps he could spare a few minutes to help her sort her tangled emotions and figure out how she was going to deal with Kevin.

A tiny ray of hope shone through the confusion. This discovery might jolt Oliver into admitting—oh, please, please, please—that he couldn't bear to lose her.

Brooke's spirits soared at the possibility.

Chapter Thirteen

Oliver spent most of Monday playing catch-up at work. That was the price of indulging himself all weekend. But it was worth it.

With so many things on his mind, he hadn't given much thought to Winston Grooms until the developer called around five o'clock. "Good news!" the man's voice rang out. "Our board has approved you for the position of vice president of international development."

Oliver scrambled to marshal his thoughts. "I didn't realize the post was officially vacant."

"I wanted to wait until I could offer you the position," the other man explained. "Things are popping. We've got a series of meetings scheduled with international prospects and I need to bring you up to speed right away. You'll be based in our Tokyo and Paris offices. You can stay at the corporation's luxury apartments."

"Impressive."

"By the way, did I mention the salary?" He cited a generous sum and made references to profit sharing and stock options.

Oliver's heart leaped. This was what he'd longed for. "I'm negotiating to sell my business, but you know how long these things take. Any chance I could start now and come up with the half million later?"

Seconds ticked by. Had his inability to invest put his future at risk?

Concern underscored the developer's response. "The board places a heavy emphasis on team spirit. Our other top managers are completely committed personally and professionally to our goals."

Oliver saw his opportunity slipping away. He decided to borrow the money, drawing on his line of credit, and repay the debt once he completed the sale of the business and the beach property. "I can arrange it in a few days. Will that be all right?"

"Can you do it by Friday?" Winston asked.

"Friday, it is."

Amid a surge of adrenaline, Oliver hung up. Matters were moving fast—maybe even a bit too fast. As a rule, he weighed risks and benefits with care. But if he delayed, he'd be the loser.

Brooke poked her nose in. She was wearing one of her many ridiculous pairs of sunglasses, these ones shaped like guitars with glitter around the edges.

As always, the sight of her filled him with delight. There was no one he'd rather share this moment with.

"Hey, great news!" He skirted the desk and caught her in a hug. "Winston Grooms wants to hire me."

"Immediately?" Her voice quavered.

"As of next week. You won't believe the salary!" At some level he registered her unhappiness, but exhilaration carried him along.

When he released her, Brooke adjusted her sunglasses. "Congratulations. Does that mean you'll be moving?"

"I'll be based in Paris and Tokyo. Can you imagine? I've always dreamed of traveling."

She fiddled with her purse strap. "I'm pleased for you."

"I'd love to bring you with me. Maybe after a while…" He stopped, unwilling to make promises he wasn't sure he could keep.

These past few days had been wonderful. He was going to miss Brooke more than he'd ever missed anyone, and he hated leaving her. How upset was she? He wished he could see her eyes behind the dark lenses.

"Once I settle into the job, I'll schedule visits," he assured her. "With luck, I can get back for the baby's birth."

She nodded dully.

Oliver's gut twisted, but he had to be realistic. "Brooke, I don't mean to run out on you. The timing's lousy. If I let this opportunity slip away, however, nothing else may come close again."

"Dr. Salonica found out about the pregnancy," she declared abruptly. "He's going to tell Kevin."

The mention of that leech's name set Oliver's teeth on edge. Still, Kevin *was* the father. "He owes you child support. That could be a benefit, at least."

"I won't accept anything from him." Brooke began to pace. Oliver stepped back to avoid a collision. "Oh, who am I fooling? I may have to."

"Don't worry about rent. You can stay at the house for free till the baby's born."

Removing the sunglasses, Brooke slanted a dubious gaze at him. "Are you saying you'll have plenty of money? This guy Winston isn't still demanding some huge investment?"

"Well, yes, I have to raise half a million. But—"

"I'll find somewhere else to stay."

Oh, damn. He'd let her down, his very best friend in the world. "That isn't necessary."

"This baby is my responsibility, not yours."

"That changed when we became lovers."

"We're friends with privileges," she corrected. "And don't you forget it. Don't bother to argue. I would never stand in the way of your dream." She ducked out before he could frame a reply.

Oliver squelched the impulse to run after her. They'd talk later this evening.

He tried not to think about the fact that time was running out for both of them.

ON THE WAY HOME Brooke tried to understand why Oliver's announcement had hit her so hard. She should have expected this. In view of his ambition, she'd known he wasn't the sticking-around kind.

Yet the prospect of losing him hurt like fire. Why had she been so foolish as to fall in love?

As if a person could control such a thing.

She had to let him go. Even if she had the power, she would never deny the man she loved something so important to him.

As she halted in front of Alice's house, her cell phone rang. For one brief moment, Brooke hoped it might be Oliver calling to say he'd changed his mind and couldn't bear to part with her.

The screen revealed the truth. It was Kevin.

Oh, fudge.

An image of the man appeared uninvited in her mind.

Ingratiating smile, star-quality dimples and rounded cheeks that in retrospect seemed immature for a man of forty-one.

Dr. Salonica hadn't wasted any time notifying his friend, she reflected grumpily. "Brooke here."

"Hey. Just heard the big news!" Phony enthusiasm infused his voice. It *had* to be phony.

"Okay…" She waited.

"I sure miss the way things used to be between us."

Perhaps he meant it. After all, she'd paid most of the bills and catered to his wishes. "I don't."

"Come on, sweetie. You aren't the type to hold a grudge," he wheedled. "Where are you staying? I could move in with you until we find a place of our own."

"I thought you'd reconciled with Laura," she said with genuine surprise.

"I had. Then Helen Salonica called."

"Already?" That woman worked fast.

"Laura just phoned, spitting nails about me having a kid with you. She's packed my bags and put them on the front porch."

He'd been kicked out. "And you thought of me?" How flattering.

"Didn't we have fun? It'll be great—you, me and the baby. You've still got your job, right?"

Brooke couldn't bear the man's presumptuousness any longer. "I'm glad you acknowledge paternity. What lawyer should I contact about child support? The same one who's handling your divorce?"

"I can't believe you're acting like such a witch. We're going to be parents. That ought to be special."

"If you insist, we'll arrange visitation rights after the

baby's born." But only if he insisted a *lot*. "Other than that and paying child support, you are out of my life."

"You can't be serious!"

"Go kneel in front of your wife and beg for forgiveness. If you're lucky, maybe she'll take you back. For your daughters' sakes, I hope so. And don't bother me again. I'm involved with someone else." Brooke pressed the end button.

She sat there, holding on to the steering wheel and shaking. Of all the idiotic things she'd done in her life, Kevin was right at the top of the list. The only good thing to come out of the relationship was this precious baby.

Where she'd found the strength to dismiss him, Brooke didn't know. Wait a minute—yes, she did. She'd found it because she was becoming a mother. And because loving Oliver had taught her what a relationship with a man could be like.

For however long it lasted.

Gingerly, she opened the car door and slid out. With all the afternoon's tense emotions, she'd tried to ignore the uncomfortable sensation in the pit of her stomach. But as she straightened up, it grew into a full-blown ache.

And it wasn't in her stomach, she now realized.

Brooke leaned against the side of the car. She *couldn't* be having problems with the pregnancy. Fear washed away all other concerns.

"Is something wrong?" Until the older woman spoke, Brooke hadn't even noticed Alice Watson retrieving mail from her mailbox a few feet away.

"It might be the baby," Brooke said.

"I'll call an ambulance." Her neighbor started toward the house.

"No!" This didn't merit such drastic treatment. "I don't

mean to cause trouble." A familiar car rolled down the street. Jane's. "Thank goodness. Here's a doctor."

"I'll fetch her." Alice hurried to explain the situation.

Jane rushed over, asked a few questions and then helped Brooke into her passenger seat. "I'm driving you to the hospital. Either Sean or I will check for bleeding and do an ultrasound."

"I'll call Oliver and fill him in," Alice promised. "Anyone else I should notify?"

Not Kevin. "Later on, I'd appreciate your telling Renée. I don't want to disturb her at the salon."

"Will do."

Brooke fastened her belt and gripped the edge of the seat. And prayed that the baby was all right.

LYING IN THE HOSPITAL bed connected to an intravenous drip, Brooke appeared small and fragile. Oliver had never felt so helpless.

He'd zipped through yellow lights, wishing he'd kept her at his office longer. He'd been in such a hurry to talk to Sandy about selling the office, he hadn't even considered that the stress might affect her pregnancy.

As it turned out, the agent could only afford a half-interest in the office and so he'd proposed a partnership. Oliver pushed aside the issue. Right now nothing else mattered but Brooke's well-being.

"I'm so sorry. I didn't mean to bring this on," he told her.

She patted his arm with her free hand. "You didn't. My placenta attached low in the uterus. The condition's called placenta previa. That's what caused the bleeding."

He wasn't sure whether to be grateful or extra worried. "Did you lose a lot of blood? Is the baby okay?"

"We're both fine. I have to stay overnight, and then it's bed rest for a week. If there's no further bleeding, Dr. Sawyer says I can go back to work."

"Thank goodness Alice and Jane were there." He appreciated his neighbors more than ever.

"Jane believes it's a girl, by the way." She smiled wanly.

"A girl," he repeated. A little Brooke, with big green eyes and cinnamon hair. She'd look adorable in a pair of child-size sunglasses. "Have you decided on a name?"

"A name?" Her mouth quivered.

"How about Rivulet? That's a *little* brook," he teased.

To his dismay, she burst into tears.

"I'm kidding." He handed her a tissue box from the table. Her hormones must be seriously out of whack. "Pick whatever name you like."

She cried harder.

Oliver sank onto the edge of the bed. "This isn't a big deal." *Okay, wise up, smart guy.* "You aren't crying about the name thing, are you?"

She gazed at him sadly. "I've been such an idiot."

Since he'd accused her of that, Oliver couldn't argue. "What brought this on?"

"I've been charging forward, assuming I could handle anything. Then, wham! Standing there in the street too scared to move pretty much put an end to that idea."

He rushed to reassure her. "But you're fine. Or you will be soon."

"Thanks to Jane and Alice, but next time they might not be around. If I can't take care of myself, how can I protect a baby?" She blew into a tissue.

Oliver supposed he should be glad she'd come to her senses. But he wasn't. "You aren't alone."

"Yes, I am, and parenting is a huge job. Some women manage, and I admire them. But I'm not them." More tears fell.

He traced the path of them down her cheek with his finger. "Brooke, you're in no condition to make decisions right now."

"I have to start thinking of what's best for the baby. You were right all along. I have to put her up for adoption." Rolling to one side, she burrowed her head into the pillow.

In a million years, Oliver could never have predicted his own response. Which was to say, "Don't be ridiculous!"

Brooke shifted until he could see her woebegone face again. "There's nothing ridiculous about it. My child deserves a family she can count on."

A yearning to shelter this woman swept everything else from Oliver's mind. "You don't have to give up your little girl," he blurted out. "Because you're going to marry *me*."

Chapter Fourteen

Although Brooke's heart leaped, she suspected she might have misheard. "Am I dreaming, or was that a proposal?"

He dabbed her cheeks with a tissue. "It was, my darling Brooke. I mean, it is. All we have to do is work out the details."

"What kind of details?" She searched his face for the answer, hoping he meant choosing a site for the wedding and the style of ring.

Brooke had grown up dreaming of a white knight who would swoop down and rescue her. As she'd grown older, she'd accepted the notion that her hero might arrive slightly tarnished. Or more than slightly.

And then she'd fallen for Oliver, a man who outshone any mythical knight. She loved, trusted and respected this man. Yearned to wake up next to him every morning, to share laughter and tears with him, and to feel joy swell in her as she watched him play with their child. Because the baby *would* become his, regardless of genetics.

Now she waited in agony while he took his time to respond. *Please love me the way I love you.*

"Here's how it would have to work," he explained. "I'll

be gone a lot, out of the country. But once we're husband and wife, I can provide a home and visit as often as possible. Maybe we won't have a conventional marriage, but who cares?"

A week ago Brooke might have jumped at the offer. For the moment Oliver could solve all her problems. Let the future take care of itself.

She longed for the person she used to be. Because, dear heaven, this man offered so much more than mere financial stability. He offered her...

His heart? Maybe a small piece of it, along with a tiny bit of his attention. Other than that, they'd be leading separate lives.

Perhaps with another man, Brooke could have accepted the situation in order to keep her baby. But not with Oliver. Of all the men she'd ever met, he alone had the power to break her heart completely.

Somewhere along the line, she'd learned to look ahead, and whichever choice she made now, the future looked bleak. At least through adoption her daughter could grow up with two parents.

Oliver was waiting for an answer. From deep within, Brooke gave him one. "No."

"Excuse me?"

"I can't marry you."

His gaze bored into hers. "Why not? Hold on—I get it."

"You do?" Was it possible he understood—and was willing to change?

"I left out the part about how much I love you. I do, Brooke. I'm sorry—I love you." His blue eyes were luminous with excitement. "Now, say yes, please?"

Disappointment choked her. "I can't."

"What did I leave out?" he pressed.

"The marriage part."

"You mean, the wedding?"

"No! I mean, being together. You aren't really offering me a marriage. I'm not sure what this would be. A long-distance contract, I suppose," she said. "Under those circumstances, I'd rather marry someone I'm indifferent to than the man I love."

Releasing her, he began to pace. "Do you have any idea how muddleheaded that sounds?"

"For once in my life, I *am* thinking clearly!" Brooke burst out. "I know what I need from a man. From you, Oliver."

He raked his fingers through his hair, leaving it mussed. "I can't believe I'm hearing this from the woman who planned to drag a virtual stranger to the altar as long as he met her minimum qualifications."

"*That* was muddleheaded," she protested. "Now listen. There was this scene in a TV show—don't make fun!— where the guy kept fighting his feelings for the woman until he couldn't stand it any longer. In the pouring rain, he stood outside her window and gazed at her with such longing that it was obvious they had to be together. That's the kind of intensity I need from you. Otherwise you'll break my heart and my daughter's, and I won't let you do that."

The vulnerability she saw in his eyes tore at her. She'd hurt him. She'd never imagined she had that kind of power over Oliver.

"I can't believe you're turning me down." His voice was close to breaking.

Brooke wished she could soothe his distress. She didn't

dare yield, though. "Oh, Oliver, I love you, too. But I can't agree to a shell of a marriage."

A sigh escaped him. "I've been building toward this opportunity all my life. I need this, Brooke."

"I admire your determination and your drive." What an ironic situation. "Aren't you glad I'm finally growing up?"

"At the expense of saying no to me?"

"Guess that's the price."

He sat down on the bed again. His arm brushed Brooke's and she had to fight not to promise him anything. "I admire you, too. But you're driving me crazy."

For a while they remained silent. She imagined Oliver was turning the situation over and over in his mind, seeking a way out, a viable compromise, and failing to find one. Just as she was doing.

At last he leaned forward and brushed a kiss across her forehead. "I'll always be your friend. I meant what I said about staying in the house for free. And if there's anything else you need... Well, I know you won't ask, so I'll check with Renée and Jane, and they'll tell me."

"Thanks." Instead of melting against him as she longed to do, she sank back into her pillow.

"I'll drive you home tomorrow, once you're released. Okay?"

She nodded, afraid she might break down if she tried to speak.

Oliver left, after explaining apologetically that he had a ton of work to do. *Of course.*

Alone, Brooke reflected on the quirks of fate. The one time she looked before she leaped, she'd been forced to reject the man she truly loved. That almost made her long to be immature again.

Someone tapped at the door. "Mind a little company?" Alice asked from the doorway.

"I'd love some."

The older woman presented her with a box of chocolates. "Hope this isn't against doctor's orders. I figured you could use some comfort food."

"Fabulous."

They each selected a chocolate. "Is it all right to ask how you're doing?"

"I'm fine. The baby, too." Brooke explained the diagnosis.

"Well, good. Then, are those tears of happiness?" Alice asked.

Her visitor seemed so gentle and so wise that Brooke let her feelings pour out. "Oliver asked me to marry him and I turned him down. He's going to be working overseas and I love him too much to have a long-distance relationship. Am I being ridiculous?"

Her guest used a tissue to wipe chocolate from her fingers. "I'm a poor one to ask. I've never been married."

"Ever fallen in love?" Brooke asked.

"Twice." Alice's mouth twisted. "I've got a lousy track record. My high-school sweetheart broke off our engagement right after graduation, joined the army and then married a woman he met in Germany. That's George. He's widowed now and he found me on the Internet last fall. In case you're wondering, I've decided not to move in with him. I'm not ready for that."

For an instant Brooke glimpsed this dignified ex-principal as a heartbroken young woman, and then her brain shifted back to the present. "Who was the other guy?"

"At twenty-four, I fell for a married man. In those days

divorce wasn't acceptable, and besides, he had children."
Alice shook her head. "I can't believe how stupid I was,
on all sorts of levels."

"Kind of like me and Kevin," Brooke murmured.

"At least you've moved on," her visitor noted. "I hung
on to that man for ten years. How lamebrained was that?"

"You must have had your reasons."

"For a woman who took so much pride in being sensible
I had quite a talent for deceiving myself." Alice's fingers
hovered over the chocolate box. Receiving an encourag-
ing look from Brooke, she helped herself to a second piece.
"I figured I had plenty of time to marry and have kids. Instead, I stayed too long at the fair. In my midthirties, I was
felled by what we used to call female problems and ended
up having a hysterectomy."

"That's awful."

"It's what I deserved. The man stuck by his wife, that
poor, long-suffering woman, but by siphoning off his
energy and affections I deprived them both of the chance
to repair their relationship. If I have a point to share with
you, Brooke, it's that we don't get an unlimited number of
chances. So use yours wisely."

Brooke refused to reconsider her decision regarding
Oliver. But she needed advice on another issue. "I'm considering giving up the baby for adoption. My life is so
unstable, I don't see how I could give her a good home."

"You should talk to Jane."

Brooke hadn't expected to hear *that*. "Why?"

"I've already said enough." Alice rose to leave. "I've
always regretted not being a grandmother. If you keep this
baby, I volunteer my services as a grandma substitute. That
includes babysitting." She qualified that. "On occasion."

"How kind."

"Actually it's rather selfish." With a wistful smile, she was gone.

Brooke hunkered down, too weary to keep her eyes open. Still, Alice's comments continued to play in her brain.

ON TUESDAY Oliver arrived at the hospital a few minutes before noon. He spotted Brooke emerging from the elevator in a wheelchair pushed by Jane McKay.

"You *did* remember I'm picking you up, didn't you?" he prompted.

Embarrassment colored Brooke's cheeks. "Jane agreed to drive me home and I forgot you'd already offered."

"You're forgiven." He was glad to see her well enough to leave this place. "No further bleeding?"

"None," Jane assured him.

"I've decided to keep the baby," Brooke said firmly. "I think I'll name her Marlene, after my mother."

What terrific news. "That's great!" Since he'd be leaving town soon, Oliver tried to figure out how else he could provide for her. "I'll arrange for a cleaning service to come in twice a month. You shouldn't have to do housework."

Brooke flushed an even deeper shade of pink. "That won't be necessary. Jane has invited me to live with her."

"I don't understand," he said. "Why?"

"When I bought a four-bedroom house, I thought I'd have a family by now. Well, it didn't work out, and frankly, I just rattle around in there all by myself," Jane admitted. "Brooke needs a place to call home and I enjoy her company. It seems like fate, don't you think?"

As they traversed the lobby, Oliver noted a change in

air pressure. His ears got stuffy and he felt a little dizzy. "I seriously doubt fate intended you to…" He stopped himself on the verge of saying *steal my girlfriend*. "Inconvenience yourself."

"It's not inconvenient at all. I adore having a baby underfoot," Jane chirped as she pushed the wheelchair toward the exit. "I can't believe she's asked me to be the godmother! It's so exciting."

"Congratulations." He paced alongside.

"Aren't you proud of me?" Brooke asked as the automatic door swung open. "I'm planning ahead."

"With a vengeance." Ruefully Oliver escorted them down a ramp. At the bottom, in a no-stopping zone, was Jane's car. Those MD plates must bring special privileges.

A sense of loss rooted him to the sidewalk as he watched Brooke slide inside. Although her practical arrangements impressed him, he'd still been hoping she might change her mind and agree to become his wife.

She didn't need him nearly as much as he'd imagined.

"See you later," Brooke called out.

"Later," he echoed.

He ought to be pleased for her.

Instead, he felt like hell.

THAT EVENING Oliver dropped by Jane's house with takeout food. He managed to exchange no more than a few private words with Brooke before Alice arrived. When he stopped by on Wednesday night, Brooke and Jane invited him to watch a chick flick starring Hugh Grant. He declined.

Did those women have to be so chummy? Except for a farewell hug, Brooke hardly seemed to notice he was around.

To add to his aggravation, on Thursday morning his

car engine developed an alarming knock. He swung by Rafe's garage.

The place was packed with vehicles awaiting service. Among all the cars, Oliver was surprised to see Sherry's luxury sedan.

His cousin strolled over, wrench in hand. Noticing the direction of Oliver's gaze, he said, "It broke down again, just as I predicted. Ms. LaSnob tried to blame me, even though I'd warned her. She also refused to have the damn thing towed to the dealer and leave me alone. By sheer luck, I got my hands on the necessary part in a hurry. Believe me, I can't wait to see the last of her."

Oliver wasn't pleased about the situation, either. "Can you work me in? I'm in a hurry."

"Family comes first," his cousin agreed. "Pop the hood, will you?"

Oliver obeyed. After listening to the engine, Rafe leaned down and tightened something. "Try it now."

Smooth as glass. "You're a genius. What do I owe you?"

"Satisfy my curiosity and we're square."

"About what?"

Rafe stretched. Judging by the smears on his blue coveralls, he'd been working hard this morning. "I heard Brooke moved in with Jane. You guys seemed so good together. I'd have sworn you'd fallen for her. What's up with that?"

None of his business. Except that Rafe *had* fixed the knock. "I asked her to marry me and she said no."

"The great Oliver Armstrong struck out? Why?"

"Because I'm not going to be around all that much." He explained Winston's offer. "It's too good to pass up."

Rafe wiped a wrench on his coverall, adding to the mess. "You're crazy enough about the woman to propose, but you'd toss her aside to work for that arrogant son-of-a-bee?"

"I know you dislike him," Oliver conceded. "But this opportunity could set me up for life."

"Yeah? I never figured I'd say this to the guy who left me in the dust all the way through school, but you're dumb as mud."

"Like hell!"

"Whatever." With a wave, his cousin sauntered off.

Oliver knew he should switch on the ignition and go his way. Rafe's reaction puzzled him, though. His cousin had never married, and in his thirty-two years he'd dated very few women who'd lasted long enough for Oliver to even remember them.

So why the heck was he giving advice to the lovelorn?

"Hey." Swinging out of his car, Oliver strode after Rafe. "Finish what you started."

His cousin spun around. "You spoiling for a fight?"

"I didn't mean it that way." He folded his arms. "You seemed to be getting at something, in your own clumsy way. So spit it out."

His cousin glanced at the waiting automobiles and apparently decided they could wait a little longer. "I know what this is about. You're afraid your dad will turn out to be right."

"What's my father got to do with this?"

"You've been trying to prove him wrong since high school. You won't be satisfied until you've made so much money you can buy and sell the rest of us."

"What're you talking about?" He'd never heard such nonsense.

"Remember when you were named a National Merit

semifinalist?" Rafe demanded. "At the next family get-together, all Uncle Otto could talk about was how great your brother was doing at the warehouse. Every time anybody congratulated you, he scoffed."

As painful memories rushed back, Oliver could hear the scorn in his dad's voice all over again. *Don't expect me to pay for some fancy college or fill out those financial-aid forms. You want to rise above your station, boy, you're going to have to do it without my help. Believe me, when you fall on your butt, you'll come crawling to me to find you a job at the warehouse.*

Without financial aid, Oliver had been forced to abandon his hopes of pursuing a degree in business. He'd earned a real-estate license, instead.

"I'm not trying to prove anything to him," he said slowly. "I enjoy what I do."

"You'd enjoy working for that ass Winston Grooms the Fifty-Seventh?" Rafe drawled. "Right now, you're your own boss. I don't understand why you'd trade what you've got for being his flunky."

"Because I refuse to be stuck with an ordinary house, a small business, a bunch of bills…" Oliver halted, hearing his own words. Maybe he *was* afraid of turning into his father.

"I guess it all boils down to what makes you happy." Having spoken his piece, Rafe headed for Sherry LaSalle's car.

As Oliver stood there, his choices began to seem a whole lot more confusing. And a whole lot clearer, too.

Chapter Fifteen

"These are fabulous. I can't believe the best caterer I've ever met is only twelve years old!" Brooke surveyed with delight the bran muffins stuffed with dates and raisins that Diane's daughter, Brittany, had brought her.

She and her stepsister, Carly, who were on spring break, had followed the example of numerous other Harmony Circle residents. No need for Jane to cook or buy food; there'd been a stream of casseroles, snacks and desserts ever since she'd left the hospital two days ago.

The exception was Renée, who, instead of food, had dropped off several shades of nail polish. "I figure that, A, pregnant women shouldn't overeat, and B, you've got nothing to do but sit around and give yourself manicures," she'd told Brooke Wednesday evening.

"I love this!"

"Also, you won't be able to reach your toenails much longer," Renée had added. "Now, dish. Is it true that Oliver proposed?"

Brooke had repeated the story. In the end, Renée said, "His loss."

"You don't mind? I mean, that he popped the question?"

Although her friend had given Brooke permission to date her ex-boyfriend, she might feel hurt that he'd fallen in love. Well, as close to falling in love as he was capable of.

Renée chuckled. "If he'd proposed to me, I'd have run for the hills. I'm not the marrying kind. It just amazes me to find out that Oliver *is*."

"Depends on how you define being married."

"Anything involving vows and a ring, regardless of how often you see the groom." Renée had left a few minutes later, insisting that Brooke get some sleep.

Good idea, because her being on bed rest didn't seem to keep visitors at bay. This morning, a policewoman had stopped by to report that the fake Gary Lincoln had pleaded guilty to assault and attempted burglary. Since he also faced a variety of charges in Utah, there'd be no bail and no chance of that scumbag paying a return visit.

A short while later the girls had arrived with their muffins. Listening to them chatter about Brittany's catering business and Carly's avid interest in photography, Brooke hoped her daughter would be as happy as these youngsters.

"I have an order for my lemon bars on Saturday," Brittany announced as they prepared to leave. "I'll bake some extra for you."

"You sure it's not too much trouble?"

"Not at all. Will you let us hold the baby after it's born?"

"My pleasure."

Brooke accompanied them to the door. She was allowed to walk short distances around the house, although no farther.

In the wake of their departure, silence descended. Lying down and closing her eyes, Brooke found herself missing Oliver with painful intensity.

He'd been sweet to her at the hospital, unable to hide his disappointment at her plan to stay with Jane. She felt certain she'd done the right thing by accepting her new friend's offer, and yet...

If only he loved her with the same intensity. If only he dreamed of her arms around him and awoke craving the sound of her voice.

Although their time together overshadowed the rest of her past, it had, in fact, lasted little more than a week. He'd never even given her a teddy bear. If he had, she'd be hugging it right now.

But he did care about her, in his way. The least she could do was offer him a memento to carry on his travels. A gift to remember her by. Something tender and intimate without being too much.

An idea hit her. Perfect. And she could order it on the Internet, a blessing for the housebound.

Nothing would substitute for being together. But she had to give him something, since he wasn't willing to accept her heart.

WHEN OLIVER RETURNED to his office from Rafe's garage, he found an unexpected visitor waiting there. What was Winston doing there a day early and without an appointment?

Talking faster than usual, the man explained that a member of the board had proposed another candidate for the vice presidency. Winston needed a commitment right away.

Oliver had an appointment at the bank this afternoon to activate his line of credit. But when he started to say so, the words stuck in his throat.

I guess it all boils down to what makes you happy.

A vision of Brooke obscured the tall blond man standing before him. No matter where he went, he'd always worry about her. Was she safe? Did she need anything?

Did she still love him?

In the few days since she'd left his house, he hadn't stopped missing her for an instant. How was he supposed to bear months or years of this?

He couldn't lose Brooke. No matter what it cost him.

Sometimes dreams changed. Sometimes they got eclipsed entirely.

"I'm sorry," he told Winston. "As it turns out, I'd be far too distracted to do a decent job."

The man scowled. "What do you mean?"

"I've decided to get married." Not quite true, but Oliver hoped it would be. "I'm going to stay right here in Brea."

Anger contorting his face, Winston smacked a fist on the desk. "You've embarrassed me in front of my board!"

What a peculiar response, and how out of character. Puzzled, Oliver said, "At least you have another candidate."

An expression of disgust flitted across the financier's smooth face. "That's your final word?"

"Afraid so."

Without a farewell, Winston stalked off. Oliver braced for a twinge, or an onslaught, of regret.

Instead, he felt as if a weight had been lifted from his shoulders. He wouldn't have to assume a major loan or sell the beach cottage or try to figure out how to run his real-estate business from afar.

Despite what Rafe believed, Oliver's dream hadn't been merely a reaction to his father's scorn. Had he gone from college into finance, as he'd dreamed, he'd have happily joined the corporate world. Instead, he'd created his own world here in Brea—and he liked it.

Despite his good mood, something about the interchange with Winston nagged at Oliver. The man had acted almost like a different person. Why had he made such a fuss about being turned down? Why come here in person, a day before the deadline he'd set for Oliver's response?

Things didn't add up.

Someone had called Winston slippery. Who was it?

Brooke, he remembered. Brooke, the most honest person he'd ever met, had sensed that something was amiss.

Troubling pieces began sliding into place. Companies didn't normally require top management to invest half a million dollars as a condition of employment. And come to think of it, the business journals he subscribed to had never mentioned Winston or his project.

He's been playing me.

Astonished at his gullibility, Oliver dropped into his chair. He'd been so impressed by the slick presentations and by Winston's association with Sherry LaSalle and her social circle that he'd neglected to run the kind of background check the investment required. He'd behaved with as much impulsiveness as Brooke at her least sensible.

Determined to do his homework at last, he picked up the phone.

BROOKE WAS SHOPPING online when Oliver called. "I need the names of anyone you think may have invested money with Winston," he said without wasting time.

She searched her memory. Helen Salonica and her husband had attended the seminar. "The Salonicas. Why?"

"I'll explain later," he said. "Gotta go."

"Wait!" She had an urgent question of her own. "What's your favorite color?"

"I'm sorry?"

"That isn't a color."

"Blue," he said.

"Dark or light?"

"Dark. Is that all?"

"Yep."

"Catch you later."

That, she thought as he clicked off, had to be the oddest phone conversation she'd ever had.

She placed her order, switched off the computer and lay on the couch for a snooze. Perhaps half an hour passed before the phone woke her. Groggily she muttered, "Hello?"

"Brooke? It's Helen Salonica."

Brooke came awake. "What can I do for you?"

A series of shaky breaths on the other end raised her fear level. Whatever had happened, it must be serious. "Are you all right?"

"Yes, thanks to you."

"What do you mean?" Brooke scooted up and shifted so that she could sit supported by the armrest.

"You saved our lives," declared her boss's wife. "Bless you!"

How should she take such a declaration? "I'm just here resting. I haven't saved anyone's life for at least a week."

"I can't begin to tell you… Well, yes, I suppose I can." Helen regained her composure. "Oliver just called my husband. I suppose you know about that."

"Something about Winston Grooms. I gave him your names. He didn't tell me what's going on, though."

"Then let me break the news." Helen clicked her tongue. "That SOB's been scamming us. All of us."

"Winston Grooms?" Although she hadn't liked him, he'd seemed such a solid, respectable figure. "How is that possible?"

"That snake took us for two hundred and fifty thousand the first round. And that wasn't enough for the creep. He also tried to hit us up for another million. And we fell for it."

"The resort isn't worth that much?"

"There is no resort. There are no offices in Paris and Tokyo. I doubt the man owns anything beyond a few suits."

Brooke had never imagined anyone capable of such duplicity. "That's awful!"

"I should have smelled a rat when he turned up the pressure this week. He had us believing this was our last chance to get rich. Nicholas was on the verge of mortgaging his business when Oliver called."

They could have lost the office? A life's work, down the drain. Brooke was glad the Salonicas and their children had been spared such an ordeal. "Thank goodness Oliver reached you in time."

"He said you told him to warn us. You have a remarkably kind heart, after all the things I accused you of." Breathlessly Helen continued, "Nicholas explained that Kevin charged those flowers. I don't understand why my husband lied—something about trying to help that heel save his marriage—but I apologize for insulting you."

"No hard feelings."

Helen hurried on. "We're still out two hundred and fifty thousand dollars. I'd never have fallen for the scheme if I hadn't trusted Sherry LaSalle. I stuck with her through that miserable divorce, and this is how she repays me? I'll never speak to her again!"

Sherry. A memory stirred of the petite blonde standing in front of her cottage, blazing at Brooke on Helen's behalf. "I'm sure she didn't lead you astray on purpose. Didn't she sink her own money into Winston's development?"

"That's why we accepted him at face value."

According to newspaper accounts, Sherry's worth amounted to almost ten million dollars. "Did he take everything? Her whole fortune?"

"I hope he sucked her dry—that's what he tried to do to us!" Helen raged. "Well, I understand you're recuperating, and I've already gabbed long enough."

After they disconnected, Brooke leaned back on the couch. How brilliant of Oliver to figure out the swindle and warn others.

But poor Sherry LaSalle! Stripped of her money, betrayed by the man she loved and tricked into misusing the people around her. How would she cope?

Brooke felt more grateful than ever for her job and her friends.

Another thought occurred to her. Oliver had been so excited about his new opportunity, and now it had evaporated, along with everything else. Although she wished this turn of events could bring him back to her, what mattered most was his happiness, and that might still involve seeking an international career with a legitimate corporation.

Refusing to worry anymore, Brooke indulged in a rare treat—watching soap operas. After dozing in front of the TV for a couple of hours, however, she had to admit they weren't half as interesting as her own life.

She was glad when Alice's face appeared at the front

window. "Stay down," she called. "I have a key." The older woman entered a moment later. "Have you seen the news?"

"I was watching the soaps."

"Pardon me." Borrowing the remote, the older woman changed to a local station. "You won't believe this."

To the newsman's left appeared a photo of Winston Grooms. "The FBI today announced a probe into the activities of this man, who goes by the name of Winston Grooms III. His real name, federal agents say, is Wally Grinnell, and he's being sought on suspicion of fraud."

Brooke stared at the television in fascination. She'd never had such a strong personal connection to a major news story before.

"According to an FBI spokeswoman, Grinnell has been under investigation for some time," the anchor went on. "The bureau decided to go public today after one of the alleged targets began alerting other possible victims."

"That's Oliver!" Brooke crowed. "He figured it out."

"The FBI should have acted sooner," Alice grumbled. "I'm sure people got fleeced in the interim."

Brooke supposed the feds had had their reasons. "Maybe they were trying to figure out where he stashed the money he stole before they took action."

"That's our Brooke. The eternal optimist." Alice patted her arm.

After a commercial break, the newscaster returned. "Grinnell is believed to have fled in a car belonging to his fiancée, Sherry LaSalle, ex-wife of well-known attorney Elliott LaSalle. His own car was picked up earlier today by the leasing agency."

After describing the vehicle, the newscaster provided details. Winston, or rather, Wally, hadn't even acquired the land he'd shown in his brochures and he'd used architectural designs of existing hotels. He was believed to have scammed in excess of twenty million dollars.

"Twenty million dollars!" gasped Lois Oldham, stepping through the open door. "All right if I come in?"

"Me, too," said Minnie Ortiz from behind her.

"I took the liberty of phoning them," Alice explained. "Hope you don't mind."

"Of course not." Brooke waved them all inside. "Let's have a party."

"I'll contact the other Foxes at work. They can bring takeout," Alice volunteered. "You have to eat, anyway."

"Great!"

Brooke would much rather Oliver had stopped by, but she didn't dare hope for a renewal of his offer. He was kind, but not truly in love the way she was, with a hunger so deep it had changed her life. He'd offered marriage to protect her, and thanks to Jane's generosity, she no longer required that protection.

Her white knight. She'd always love him, no matter where he went.

The arrival of more Foxes provided a welcome distraction. Voices buzzed and the topic soon turned to the historic cottage.

"They won't be tearing it down!" crowed Cynthia Lieberman, the psychologist.

"I bet Sherry'll put it up for sale," suggested Lois as she tugged a crochet hook through a colorful square.

"Maybe she'll move in." Minnie's eyes twinkled. "She owns the cottage in her own name. That might be all she's got left."

"Across the street from Rafe? We'll be seeing fireworks

for sure," whooped Sarah, who'd brought a bucket of fried chicken with her.

"I feel sorry for her," Brooke told the group. "The guy ripped her off and broke her heart."

Tess Phipps brandished a chicken wing. "Have you forgotten the way she sneered at us? This seems like a well-deserved lesson in humility."

Alice handed Brooke a napkin to save her reaching for it. "I hope you never get tough and cynical like the rest of us."

"*I* feel sorry for Sherry, too." Jane handed more napkins around. "Well, a tiny bit."

"A tiny bit, to match our tiny houses?" Tess joked. "She'll never live down that remark."

Amid laughter, everyone dug into the food as they watched a profile of Wally Grinnell. Rather than being the scion of a wealthy New York family and a graduate of Harvard Business School as he'd claimed, he was a junior-college dropout from New Jersey, son of a politician father who'd been convicted of taking bribes.

"The fruit doesn't fall far from the tree," Lois observed.

A newsman interviewed a forlorn employee on a sidewalk outside Winston's office in Fullerton. "My last paycheck bounced," she complained. "Turns out he owes rent and the furniture was leased. I've got kids to support. What am I supposed to do? The guy stole twenty million dollars and he was too greedy to pay a few bills with it."

To the camera the reporter said, "Grinnell's fiancée, Sherry LaSalle, a major investor in his sham business, remains in seclusion. Her attorney assures us she will pay employees with what little money remains."

"That's decent," Jane noted. "I hope she's okay."

"She'll land on her feet," Tess said. "Probably snare another snobby rich guy before her bed gets cold."

Brooke doubted Sherry would trust another man in a hurry. On the other hand, what options did she have?

Outside, the sun was setting. Once again Brooke thought of Oliver, but perhaps he was closeted with FBI agents. Maybe he'd stop by later tonight—with luck, after all these women had gone home.

In the kitchen, the phone rang. Jane excused herself, while the others continued watching the program. After a moment Brooke heard the door to the garage open.

"What's Jane doing?" she wondered aloud.

"Maybe she left something in her car," Sarah said.

"Speaking of cars…" Lois pointed at the screen, where Rafe's familiar face appeared next to a truck with its hood propped open. He must be working late at the garage, unless this had been taped earlier.

"I had no idea he planned to steal her Mercedes," the mechanic told the reporter. "Mrs. LaSalle was supposed to pick it up at my garage. When Winston arrived, he said he was acting on her behalf. He wrote me a check and I handed him the keys."

"Going to try depositing that check?" asked an off-screen female voice.

Rafe shook his head. "Why bother? The bank'll charge me when it bounces."

"Hey!" Sarah peered out the window. "Jane's sprinklers just came on. Why's she watering her lawn right now?"

"Maybe she thinks we'd enjoy a swim on the way home," Alice teased.

"Jane?" Lois called as their hostess reappeared. "Did you know…?"

"It's all right. Wait and see." Jane bestowed a mysterious smile on them.

Sarah remained glued to the window. "There's a guy out there. Is he supposed to adjust your sprinkler heads?"

"Not exactly."

Cynthia followed her gaze. "He's getting wet. Wait a minute—that's Oliver!"

"What?" Before Brooke could get up, her cell phone rang. "Hello?"

"Can you step into the doorway for a minute?" Oliver asked.

"What're you doing?" As she started to rise, two women caught her elbows and boosted her.

"Better hurry. Getting wet isn't good for my phone."

Jane held the door wide. Obviously she was in on the gag.

Waving away further offers of help, Brooke padded forward. Couldn't Oliver find a less public way to act silly? Still, her spirits soared at the prospect of seeing him.

Outside, in a rainbow-hued spray of water, stood the man Brooke loved. He wasn't laughing. In fact, he looked dead earnest.

When he dropped to his knees, she realized he hadn't been joking at all.

Chapter Sixteen

"What's going on?" Brooke stepped outside, disregarding her state of undress, since by now half the neighborhood was acquainted with her flowered bathrobe.

"Careful," Jane cautioned from within.

Ah, yes. Bed rest. Brooke sank onto the front step, clear of the spray, and waited.

A dozen feet away Oliver had positioned himself right where the jets collided. Hair plastered to his head and water dripping down his shirt, he clasped his hands over his heart.

"Remember that TV show?" he called.

Why was he babbling about television? "What show?"

"The guy standing in the rain."

She searched for the right association. "Gene Kelly?"

"Not singing. Standing. That romantic scene you described."

"Oh. It was an episode from *Roswell.*" With a jolt, Brooke got the point. "That's why you're in the sprinklers?"

"If I waited for the next rain in Southern California, the baby might be graduating from high school."

He'd done this to please her! Even more thrilling, he'd gone down on his knees in front of the whole world. Faces must be plastered against every inch of Jane's front windows.

Despite an almost painful surge of hope, Brooke worried about his welfare. "You should come out of there. You must be soaking."

"Wait till I finish." From his pocket Oliver drew a velvet jeweler's box. "Brooke Bernard, will you—"

Oh, Lord! Another proposal—exactly what she yearned for with her entire being. Yet she couldn't let him proceed for the wrong reasons. "Wait. Is this because… I understand how wrenching it is that Winston lied about the job. But I can't be your consolation prize."

"Consolation prize?" He blinked away a stream of water. "Brooke, I turned him down."

"You mean…before?"

"Absolutely." He sheltered the velvet box with his torso. "I couldn't leave you. Even if he'd been on the level, accepting his offer would have ruined my chance of happiness."

This is too good to be true. "When did you figure out what a ripoff artist he was?"

"After I gave him the news that I wasn't putting half a million dollars in his hot, little hands. His reaction seemed odd. That's what tipped me off."

Oliver had rejected the offer because he loved her. Incredible.

Wonderful.

She grinned. "You're staying! Promise?"

"Yes. I'll be right here. In fact, this whole situation may work to my advantage. Now that I've taken on a business partner, we've got great ideas for expanding. We—"

Jane interrupted. "Haven't you wandered off topic?"

"Sorry!" Oliver cleared his throat. "Brooke, before I drown, will you marry me? I love you more than money. I love you more than ambition. I even love your teddy bears and your ridiculous sunglasses. Will you marry me forever?"

"Yes." Afraid he might not hear her over the noise of the sprinklers, she shouted, "Yes, yes, yes!"

Inside, applause broke out. Down the street, she spotted Rafe Montoya in his yard, snapping shots on his cellphone camera. He paused long enough to pump a fist in approval.

"I'm turning off the sprinklers now," Jane announced, and went inside. Brooke heard her scolding the others to give them privacy, as if that was possible in the front yard.

Oliver sprang up and splashed across the grass. "I want to share every remaining minute of your pregnancy. We'll attend childbirth classes and shop for baby furniture, and I'm going to become such an expert on babies that women for hundreds of miles will seek my advice. I'll tell them, no, I'm only doing this for Brooke."

She launched herself into his arms, hit him with a squish and wrapped him so tight he couldn't escape. Judging by the enthusiasm with which he was kissing her, he had no desire to do that.

CONCERNED ABOUT her pregnancy, Oliver carried Brooke inside. "Do you feel okay? This might be too much activity."

"I'm fine. Better than fine!"

Behind them, the sprinklers faded to silence. Indoors, a knot of women fussed over Brooke, while Oliver mopped off with Jane's towels.

Everyone admired the ring he'd slipped onto Brooke's finger. A bit loose, but the jeweler had agreed to size it.

Oliver yearned to hug her again. However, this kneeling-in-the-rain business had its drawbacks, such as leaving him drenched.

Alice took charge. "You go home and change," she commanded. "Brooke needs to throw on something dry, too."

After an exchange of longing gazes with his bride-to-be, he reluctantly obeyed. When he returned, Brooke had been bundled into a sweatshirt and loose jeans. Oliver dropped onto the couch and pulled her onto his lap. Never mind the audience. They'd become part of the scene.

"It's beautiful." She extended her left hand, where the diamond sparkled. "I'm so happy."

"Me, too." Resting his cheek against the top of her head, he surveyed the gathering of Foxes. "Isn't this fun? An instant engagement party."

"What about the wedding?" Minnie asked.

"Brooke's in no shape to plan that," Alice said.

"Have you picked a date?" Cynthia inquired. "I can find out whether the clubhouse is available."

"Bart grows tons of flowers," added Tess. "I'm good at arrangements."

"I know a secondhand shop that specializes in wedding dresses." Sarah frowned as faces turned toward her with varying degrees of curiosity. "I wasn't looking for myself. A friend got married last year."

"If it's okay with Brooke, I'd rather not wait very long," Oliver told them. Personally he'd prefer to march down to the county courthouse tomorrow, if the doctors agreed.

Brooke released a contented sigh. "The sooner, the better."

All day, fear had dogged Oliver—that he'd blown his chances, that she'd reject this proposal as readily as the first one. She'd been right to turn him down then. Although his heart had been in it, his soul hadn't.

Now, she had them both. And always would.

THE MAY WEDDING of Brooke Bernard and Oliver Armstrong was the high point of the Harmony Circle social season. Of course, the only other major social events were community potlucks, but lots of people hoped this might set a precedent.

As far as anyone recalled, there'd never before been a wedding at the clubhouse. In any case, there couldn't have been a prettier one. Outside, clouds of lavender blossoms covered the jacaranda trees, and they were mirrored inside the clubhouse by the silver-and-lavender flower arrangements and bridesmaid dresses.

Jane McKay, co-maid of honor with Renée Trent, looked forward to welcoming her goddaughter in October. She was grateful that the pregnancy was progressing well. And that Kevin, when he learned about the engagement, had signed papers relinquishing his paternity rights—and, of course, freeing him from any financial obligations.

Alongside Jane, Renée maintained a stately stride down the aisle, her thoughts on the flowers she'd woven into the bride's hair while creating an upswept coiffure. If Brooke could refrain from skipping, perhaps those petals wouldn't wind up littering the church.

Among the onlookers, Lois wept, remembering the joy of her own wedding more than thirty years earlier. Beside her, Alice shed a few tears, but she couldn't have said why—for old love affairs? For opportunities missed? Or for simple joy?

Diane Lorenz took in the excitement shining on her daughters' faces. If Brooke found as much happiness as Diane had in her new-minted marriage to Josh, she'd be a very lucky bride indeed.

The music swelled. The bride glided toward the altar on the arm of her boss, Dr. Salonica. In the audience, Helen released the last lingering suspicion she'd entertained about her husband and this pretty young woman. Brooke had eyes only for her groom, while the orthodontist exuded all the pride of a man giving away his own daughter.

While everyone else focused on the bride's radiant smile, one woman's attention fixed on the handsome man waiting in a tuxedo. Angela Chavez Armstrong burst with pride for her son. She'd come to adore her future daughter-in-law and to admire Oliver's unqualified acceptance of this baby. For years, she'd feared that his pursuit of success would destroy his capacity for love. Thank heaven she'd been wrong.

And what a joy to see him reconciled with his father. News reports lauding Oliver as a whistle-blower had won Otto's unreserved support. At last night's dinner, her husband, whose best friend had lost his retirement savings to a charlatan, had clapped the groom on the shoulder and called him a hero.

"It pays to be smart," he'd announced to the guests, "and my boy's the smartest."

Now, at the altar, the orthodontist released his charge to Oliver's care. When the bride and groom caught each other's hands, Angela could have sworn the light in the room brightened until it blotted out everything except those two blissful figures.

Which was precisely as it should be.

"I DID SAY DARK BLUE," Oliver conceded. "I don't recall mentioning anything about stars."

"Don't you think they're cute?" Brooke gave a little bounce on the bed.

He gazed down at the gift his bride had presented him on their wedding night. She'd ordered the pajamas on the Internet the day he discovered Winston's treachery, she'd explained. "Cute? Let's just say that I consider any gift from you beautiful beyond belief."

"You can toss away those black ones," she prompted. "I'm not jealous of Renée or anything. It just seems inappropriate for you to wear them, now that we're married."

"Point taken." He'd never been crazy about wearing black to bed, anyway. "Can I get naked now?"

"Sure, if you let me watch."

He laughed at her eagerness. "Better yet, remove my boxers yourself."

"You know I can't for another few months."

"Can't see me naked?"

"Well, the doctors didn't forbid *that!*" A stretching motion pulled her silky nightgown suggestively over her voluptuous shape. Oliver didn't see how he was going to bear waiting until after the baby's birth. Still, safety first.

"Here's a better idea. Let's have a pajama party on the beach." Catching her approving nod, he stripped off his underwear and donned the dark blue pajamas.

He shuddered to think how close he'd come to sacrificing this bungalow at the shore, to losing nearly everything else, as well. Instead, thanks to Brooke and his best instincts, he'd landed on his feet.

The FBI still hadn't captured Wally Grinnell. But although the con man had left behind a mess for other people, Oliver's new partnership with Sandy Rivers meant that Archway Real Estate could open a second office. His financial future looked better every day.

As for his personal future, it started right here.

Taking his wife's hand, Oliver escorted her through the cozy house and onto the front porch, which overlooked a broad expanse of beach. At this late hour, no one but a few joggers disturbed their solitude.

"This is close enough. Let's sleep here," Brooke murmured. "Sand is more romantic in the abstract than when it's stuck between your toes. Or up your…nightgown."

"Right you are." Settling onto the glider, Oliver drew her close and pulled a crocheted throw, a wedding gift from Lois, across their knees.

In front of them gleamed the starlit Pacific Ocean. Far away, it lapped at the shores of Japan and Australia and a million other places. Someday perhaps they'd explore them, Oliver mused.

In the meantime, he and his wife and their unborn daughter had much bigger adventures to look forward to. And he didn't intend to miss a moment.

* * * * *

Come back to
HARMONY CIRCLE
in January 2009 for Jacqueline Diamond's
MILLION-DOLLAR NANNY,
only from Harlequin American Romance!

The Colton family is back!
Enjoy a sneak preview of
COLTON'S SECRET SERVICE
by Marie Ferrarella,
part of
THE COLTONS: FAMILY FIRST *miniseries.*

Available from Silhouette Romantic Suspense
in September 2008.

He cautioned himself to be leery. He was human and he'd been conned before. But never by anyone nearly so attractive. Never by anyone he'd felt so attracted to.

In her defense, Nick supposed that Georgie could actually be telling him the truth. That she was a victim in all this. He had his people back in California checking her out, to make sure she was who she said she was and had, as she claimed, not even been near a computer but on the road these last few months that the threats had been made.

In the meantime, he was doing his own checking out. Up close and exceedingly personal. So personal he could feel his blood stirring.

It had been a long time since he'd thought of himself as anything other than a law enforcement agent of one type or other. But Georgeann Grady made him remember that beneath the oaths he had taken and his devotion to duty, there beat the heart of a man.

A man who'd been far too long without the touch of a woman.

He watched as the light from the fireplace caressed the outline of Georgie's small, trim, jean-clad body as she moved about the rustic living room that could have easily come off the set of a Hollywood Western. Except that it was genuine.

As genuine as she claimed to be?

Something inside of him hoped so.

He wasn't supposed to be taking sides. His only interest in being here was to guarantee Senator Joe Colton's safety as the latter continued to make his bid for the presidency. Everything else was supposed to be secondary, but, Nick had to silently admit, that was just a wee bit hard to remember right now.

Earlier, before she'd put her precocious handful of a daughter to bed, Georgie had fed his appetite by whipping up some kind of a delicious concoction out of the vegetables she'd pulled from her garden. Vegetables that, by all rights, should have been withered and dried. She'd mentioned that a friend came by on occasion to weed and tend it. Still, it surprised him that somehow she'd managed to make something mouthwatering out of it.

Almost as mouthwatering as she looked to him right at this moment.

Again, he was reminded of the appetite that hadn't been fed, hadn't been satisfied.

And wasn't going to be, Nick sternly told himself. At least not now. Maybe later, when things took on a more definite shape and all the questions in his head were answered to his satisfaction, there would be time to explore this feeling. This woman. But not now.

Dammit.

"Sorry about the lack of light," Georgie said, breaking into his train of thought as she turned around to face him. If she noticed the way he was looking at her, she gave no indication. "But I don't see a point in paying for electricity if I'm not going to be here. Besides, Emmie really enjoys camping out. She likes roughing it."

"And you?" Nick asked, moving closer to her, so close that a whisper would have trouble fitting in. "What do you like?"

The very breath stopped in Georgie's throat as she looked up at him.

"I think you've got a fair shot of guessing that one," she told him softly.

* * * * *

Be sure to look for
COLTON'S SECRET SERVICE
and the other following titles from
THE COLTONS: FAMILY FIRST *miniseries:*

RANCHER'S REDEMPTION
by Beth Cornelison
THE SHERIFF'S AMNESIAC BRIDE
by Linda Conrad
SOLDIER'S SECRET CHILD
by Caridad Piñeiro
BABY'S WATCH
by Justine Davis
A HERO OF HER OWN
by Carla Cassidy

Romantic
SUSPENSE

Sparked by Danger,
Fueled by Passion.

The Coltons Are Back!

Marie Ferrarella
Colton's Secret Service

The Coltons: Family First

On a mission to protect a senator, Secret Service agent
Nick Sheffield tracks down a threatening message only
to discover Georgie Gradie Colton, a rodeo-riding single
mom, who insists on her innocence. Nick is instantly
taken with the feisty redhead, but vows not to let his
feelings interfere with his mission. Now he must figure
out if this woman is conning him or if he can trust her
and the passion they share....

Available September wherever books are sold.

Look for upcoming Colton titles
from Silhouette Romantic Suspense:

RANCHER'S REDEMPTION by Beth Cornelison, Available October
THE SHERIFF'S AMNESIAC BRIDE by Linda Conrad, Available November
SOLDIER'S SECRET CHILD by Caridad Piñeiro, Available December
BABY'S WATCH by Justine Davis, Available January 2009
A HERO OF HER OWN by Carla Cassidy, Available February 2009

Visit Silhouette Books at www.eHarlequin.com SRS27598

NEW YORK TIMES BESTSELLING AUTHOR
SUSAN WIGGS

With her marriage in the rearview mirror, Sarah flees to her
hometown, a place she couldn't wait to leave. Now she finds
herself revisiting the past—a distant father and the unanswered
questions left by her mother's death. As she comes to terms with
her lost marriage, Sarah encounters a man she never expected to
meet again: Will Bonner, her high-school heartthrob. Now a local
firefighter, he's been through some changes himself. But just as her
heart opens, Sarah discovers she is pregnant—with her ex's twins.

It's hardly the most traditional of new beginnings, but who says life
or love are predictable…or perfect?

Just Breathe

"Susan Wiggs paints
the details of human
relationships with the
finesse of a master."
—*New York Times*
bestselling author
Jodi Picoult

*Available the first
week of September 2008
wherever hardcovers
are sold!*

MIRA®

www.MIRABooks.com   MSW2577

REQUEST YOUR FREE BOOKS!

2 FREE NOVELS PLUS 2
FREE GIFTS!

Heart, Home & Happiness!

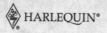

#1 *New York Times* Bestselling Author

DEBBIE MACOMBER

Dear Reader,

I have something to confide in you. I think my husband, Dave, might be having an affair. I found an earring in his pocket, and it's not mine.

You see, he's a pastor. And a good man. I can't believe he's guilty of anything, but why won't he tell me where he's been when he comes home so late?

Reader, I'd love to hear what you think. So come on in and join me for a cup of tea.

Emily Flemming

8 Sandpiper Way

On sale August 26, 2008!

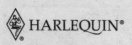
COMING NEXT MONTH

#1225 A DAD FOR HER TWINS by Tanya Michaels
The State of Parenthood
Kenzie Green is starting over—new job, new city, new house—to provide a better life for her nine-year-old twins. Unfortunately, the house isn't finished yet, so the three of them temporarily move into an apartment across the hall from the mysterious and gorgeous Jonathan Trelauney. Watching her kids open up to JT is enthralling...thinking of him as a father to her twins is irresistible!

#1226 TEXAS HEIR by Linda Warren
Cari Michaels has been in love with the newly engaged Reed Preston, CEO and heir to a family-owned Texas chain of department stores, for a long time. When their plane crashes in desolate west Texas—and help doesn't arrive—they start the long trek to civilization. Once they're rescued, will Reed follow through with his engagement...or marry the woman who has captured his heart?

#1227 SMOKY MOUNTAIN HOME by Lynnette Kent
Ruth Ann Blakely has worked in the stables at The Hawksridge School for most of her life. Her attachment to the students she teaches, to her horses and to the stables themselves is unshakeable. So when architect Jonah Granger is hired to build new a stable for the school—and tear the old one down—he's in for a fight. But Jonah isn't a man who's easy to say no to....

#1228 A FIREFIGHTER IN THE FAMILY by Trish Milburn
When Miranda "Randi" Cooke is assigned to investigate a fire in her hometown, she not only has to face her estranged family but also her ex-boyfriend Zac Parker. As the case heats up, Randi finds she needs Zac's help. While they're working closely together, her feelings for Zac are rekindled—but can the tough arson investigator forgive old hurts and learn to trust again?

www.eHarlequin.com

HARCNM0808